A Novel

I0673718

ANIMALIAN
THE SANCTUARY'S REVENGE

BOOK I

GUSTAVO CARVALHO

ISBN: 979-8-9880250-0-9
First edition, 2023
Published by Whimsy Frog LLC
Printed in United States

Gustavo Carvalho
Web: www.animalian.world
Email: contact@animalian.world
Instagram: @animalian.book

Whimsy Frog

Dedicated to my beloved wife Isis and my two amazing kids, Antonio and Adrian.

You are the light of my life and the reason I wake up every day with a smile on my face. Your love and support has given me the strength to chase my dreams and pursue my passions.
This book is a testament to the endless love and joy that you bring into my life. I am forever grateful for the memories we have created together and for the endless laughter and love that we share.

I love you now and forever.

PROLOGUE

The Sanctuary stood silent and still under the silver light of the full moon. The tall trees loomed like sentinels, watching over the school. The night was calm and peaceful, but there was a tone of unease in the air, as if something sinister was lurking just beyond the edge of the light. The silence was broken only by the soft rustling of the leaves in the wind and the occasional hoot of an owl.

Under the light of the full moon, a mysterious figure stood at a distance from the walls of the Sanctuary. The shadows obscured their face, but the gleam in their eye was unmistakable - a fierce determination to seek revenge and fulfill a thirst for vengeance.

The figure's thoughts were consumed with past injustices and slights. They remembered all the people who had wronged them, those who had belittled and made fun of their abilities. They felt the anger and resentment boiling inside them, the pain of being left behind, of feeling inferior.

"They will pay," the figure whispered to themselves, a sinister smile spreading across their face. "I will show them all what it means to cross me. I will be the one to bring them to their knees," the figure thought, the smile on their face growing wider. "They will regret ever messing with me. They will regret ever thinking they were better than me."

The figure stood there for a moment longer, lost in thought, before turning and disappearing into the night, ready to put their plans into motion.

CHAPTER 1

THE DIFFERENT ONE

❖

Ethan sat alone at lunch, staring blankly at the food on his tray. It was a typical Wednesday, and he had grown used to eating by himself, ever since he was a kid. He would usually spend his lunch period lost in his own thoughts, tuning out the noise and chatter of the other students around him. He didn't mind it much, though. He preferred his own company to that of the other kids. They always made fun of him, calling him names like "creep" and "freak", teasing him for being weird and not fitting in. He didn't understand them, and they didn't understand him.

He had always felt like he didn't belong, like he was different from everyone else. He didn't know why, but he had always felt a sense of disconnection with the world around him, as if he were a stranger in his own life.

He had a fascination for the birds that flew overhead, and he often wondered what it would be like to fly. He would spend hours watching them, trying to understand how they managed to stay in the air. But as he grew older, he learned to push those thoughts aside and focus on more practical things.

During lunch, one of the other students, a tall jock named Brad, decided to play a prank on Ethan. Brad had always been one of the kids who liked to make fun of Ethan, and today was no different. Brad and his friends approached Ethan's table, and Brad pretended to trip, causing his tray of food to fly into the air and land all over Ethan. The other students erupted in laughter, and Ethan sat there, covered in food, feeling embarrassed and humiliated. He gathered his things and left the lunchroom, his face red with anger and embarrassment. He knew he would never fit in with the other kids, and he didn't want to be a part of their cruel and thoughtless world.

After Ethan left the lunchroom, he walked to the playground to clear his head. He sat on a bench and let out a sigh. He had always felt out of place, but today's incident had made him feel even more alone. He knew that he would always be an outsider, and the thought made him feel sad and helpless.

As he sat there, lost in thought, he heard a commotion nearby. He looked up to see a group of birds flying erratically, their cries filling the air. Ethan felt a sudden urge to join them, to fly with them and escape his problems. He closed his eyes and concentrated, and suddenly, he felt himself lifting off the ground. But it was just his imagination, he opened his eyes and he was still sitting on the bench. Even though the experience felt real and exhilarating, he knew that he couldn't fly. He couldn't understand why he had felt that way, but it left him contemplating about what had just happened. He couldn't shake off the feeling that something was different, that he had some sort of power, even though he couldn't quite put his finger on what it was.

After school, Ethan made his way home. He lived in a small house with his parents, who were both ordinary people. They had always been supportive of him, but they didn't understand his feelings of alienation. He had inherited his mother's brown hair and his father's green eyes, and he was tall for his age, having recently turned 13. He was a bit lanky, but he had recently started to fill out and gain some muscle.

As he walked into his house, his mother greeted him with a smile. "How was school, dear?" she asked. Ethan shrugged and mumbled something about it being fine. He didn't feel like talking about the incident at school, and he knew his mother would just worry if she knew.

Ethan was a solitary person, and photography had been his passion for as long as he could remember. He loved to capture the beauty of nature and birds, and he had a natural talent for it. He would often spend hours wandering around the city, taking pictures of anything that caught his eye, from the birds at the park to the city's architecture. He had a keen eye for detail and composition, and he was always looking for new and interesting perspectives.

As he entered his room, he was greeted by the walls covered with his photographs. He had taken the photos he liked the most and framed them, creating a collage of his best works. Each photograph told a different story and each one had a special meaning to him. His bed was located in the middle of the room, and it was surrounded by the photographs that he had taken of birds and nature, a subject that he particularly loved. He sat on his bed and looked around his room, feeling a sense of pride and accomplishment.

Ethan grabbed his camera and walked out of his room. He needed to clear his head, and photography was the best way for him to do it. He walked around the city, taking pictures of anything that caught his eye. He started by taking shots of the birds at the park, focusing on capturing their beauty and grace as they flew through the sky. He then moved on to take pictures of the city's architecture, capturing the intricate details of the buildings and the way the light played off of them.

Ethan liked to take pictures of strangers too, as he thought it would help him understand people better. He was especially drawn to capturing the unique and interesting personalities of people from all walks of life. As he walked around the city, he saw many different people, each with their own unique characteristics.

He saw a young mother struggling to push a stroller up a hill. She was sweating and her face was contorted in a look of determination. Ethan took a picture of her, thinking that it would make for an interesting shot. He also saw an old man sitting on a bench, feeding the pigeons. The man had a kind face and a gentle smile, and Ethan thought that would make a great portrait.

As Ethan walked around the city, he came across the same group of bullies from school. The leader of the group, a tall and muscular boy, spotted Ethan and called out to him.

"Hey, look who we have here," he said with a smirk. "It's the freak from school."

The other bullies laughed and joined in, taunting and mocking Ethan.

"What are you doing here, freak? Thought you'd be hiding in a cave or something," one of them said.

Ethan replied, "I'm not hiding from anyone. I'm just doing my own thing, unlike you guys who seem to have nothing better to do than pick on others."

The leader of the group sneered at Ethan "What are you going to do about it? Cry to your mommy?"

Ethan didn't back down, "I don't have to. I have something you'll never have, dignity."

The teasing turned into a heated discussion, and soon the group of bullies started to get aggressive towards Ethan. They pushed him around and threatened him. Ethan felt trapped and didn't know what to do.

Just as things were getting out of hand, a man appeared out of nowhere. He was a tall and muscular man with short, dark hair and brown eyes, and his brown skin glistened in the sun. He was dressed in all-black clothing, including a long-sleeved shirt, pants and boots, with a hood pulled up over his head. He stepped in between Ethan and the bullies, and with a stern voice, he said, "Leave him alone."

The leader of the group sneered at the man "Who the hell are you? This doesn't concern you."

The man didn't answer, he just gave a cold look at the group, who were taken aback by his sudden appearance and were intimidated by his imposing presence. They quickly backed off and ran away, leaving Ethan and the man alone on the street. The man looked at Ethan with a kind and understanding gaze, and Ethan felt a sense of relief wash over him. He knew that he was safe now, and he felt grateful to the man for saving him. He couldn't quite put his finger on it, but there was something about him that seemed familiar. He carried himself with a sense of authority and confidence, and Ethan immediately felt respect for him.

"Thank you," Ethan said, still trying to catch his breath. "You saved me."

The man looked at Ethan with a kind and understanding gaze. "You're welcome, son," he said, in a deep and gravelly voice. "I couldn't just stand by and watch those bullies hurt you."

CHAPTER 2

A NEW WORLD AWAITS

Ethan couldn't shake off the strange encounter with the mysterious man, but as he continued to wander the city, taking in its sights and sounds, he started to put it out of his mind. He lifted his camera to his eye, capturing the vibrant colors of the bustling streets, the old school buildings, and the smiling faces of the people he encountered.

As he walked, he eventually stumbled upon an arcade and decided to take a break from exploring. The bright lights and sounds of the games were a welcome distraction, and he spent the next hour or so testing his skills on the various machines. He was especially fond of the racing game, where he found himself lost in the thrill of the competition, feeling as though he was truly behind the wheel of a high-speed car.

When the sun began to set, Ethan realized it was time to head home. He stepped back out into the city and felt a sense of peace. He had experienced a day full of adventure, mystery, fun, and even danger. Somehow that last part was exciting to him.

Ethan stepped into his home, and as soon as he walked through the front door, his mother called out to him from the living room, "Ethan, come here, we have a visitor!"

Curious, Ethan made his way to the living room, where he was shocked to see his dad talking to the same tall, muscular man he encountered before. They were sitting on the couch, sipping on a cup of coffee. It was clear that they had been chatting for some time.

Ethan's heart raced as he wondered what was going on. Had the man come to reprimand him for something? Was he in trouble? All these thoughts and more swirled through Ethan's mind as he approached the couch, feeling a mix of fear and uncertainty.

The man extended his hand, "I'm Robert Black, but feel free to address me as Mr. Black," he chuckled.

"Hi there," Ethan said, trying to sound casual. "I'm Ethan. May I ask what brings you here today?"

Mr. Black fixed his piercing gaze on Ethan, his eyes seeming to see right through him. "I've come to speak with you, Ethan," he said, his deep voice echoing in the room. "You have a special gift, and I think it's time for you to learn how to use it."

Ethan's heart skipped a beat, "Wait, what?"

Mr. Black looked at Ethan intently, "I want to introduce you to a world that most people don't know exists. A world of people like us, people with special abilities."

Ethan's mind was racing, "Special abilities? What do you mean?"

Mr. Black looked at Ethan with a serious expression, "I mean that you are an Animalian, Ethan. And I am here to invite you to the Sanctuary, where you can learn to harness and control your powers."

Ethan couldn't believe what he was hearing, "Animalian? Sanctuary? I don't understand."

Mr. Black smiled again, "I know this is a lot to take in, Ethan. But I promise you, it will all make sense once you see it for yourself. Are you ready to take the first step on a journey that will change your life forever?"

Ethan looked at Mr. Black, not knowing what to say. He had a million questions, but he had a feeling that this may be an opportunity of a lifetime. He took a deep breath and nodded, "Yes. I'm ready."

Ethan's parents were still skeptical, but they listened intently as Mr. Black spoke. He explained that Animalians were people who had inherited special powers from animals, and that the Sanctuary was a secret school where Animalians could learn to control and use their powers in the real world.

Ethan listened intently, his mind reeling with the possibilities. He had always felt different from other people, and the idea that there were others like him was both exciting and a little bit scary.

"Mr. Black," Ethan began tentatively, "you said that I'm an Animalian and that I have special abilities. Can you tell me more about it?"

Mr. Black nodded understandingly, "Of course, Ethan. Every Animalian has unique talents, but it takes time and training to discover and control them. However, I can sense that you have a strong connection to the animal kingdom, it's obvious that you have powers related to animals."

Ethan's heart began to race with excitement and curiosity, "Really? What kind of powers?"

Mr. Black smiled mysteriously, "I can't tell you for sure, but I can assure you that the Sanctuary will help you to discover and develop your abilities. We have a team of experienced teachers who will guide you every step of the way."

Ethan thought for a moment, "What about my family and friends? How will this affect them?"

Mr. Black's expression softened, "I understand your concerns, Ethan. The Sanctuary is a safe and secret place. Your loved ones will not be in danger and you will be able to contact them whenever you want. And, eventually, you will be able to use your talents to help others, including your family and friends."

Ethan continuing, "Can you tell me more about this Animalian world? How many of them are there? How do they live among humans without being discovered? And where did they come from? How did they get these powers?"

Mr. Black leaned back in his seat and gave a small chuckle, "Those are all great questions, Ethan. We are scattered all over the world, living among humans, but keeping our abilities hidden. The Sanctuary is where we come together to learn, train and connect with other like-minded individuals. As for where we came from, it is believed that the first Animalians were born out of a unique genetic mutation, a blending of human and animal DNA that resulted in the development of these special powers."

Ethan nodded, taking in this information. "And what about the outside world? How do they protect themselves and their secret?"

Mr. Black's expression grew serious, "It's not always easy, Ethan. There are those who seek to exploit or harm Animalians for their own gain. But that's why the Sanctuary exists, to teach you how to control and use your powers for self-defense and protect yourself and others. And we have a strong network of support and protection among the Animalian community. We look out for each other."

Ethan's parents, Amanda and John, were still skeptical about the existence of the Animalian world and the purpose of the Sanctuary. Amanda expressed her concerns about the safety of the school and the kind of people that Ethan would be associating with. She said, "I've never heard of such a thing, a school for people with special abilities. How do we know it's safe for Ethan? And what kind of people will he be around there?"

Mr. Black understood the concerns and reassured them, "I understand your worries, Mrs. Thompson. The Sanctuary is a safe and secure place, we have strict security measures in place to ensure the safety of our students. And as for the kind of people, they are just like Ethan, young people with special abilities, looking to learn and grow in a supportive and understanding environment."

John, Ethan's father, was worried about the financial aspect of the school, he said "It's all very intriguing, but what about the cost? Can we afford to send Ethan to this school?"

Mr. Black smiled and replied, "Don't worry about the cost, Mr. Thompson. The Sanctuary is completely free for all Animalians. And to prove to you that this is real, let me show you a demonstration of my abilities." With that, Mr. Black walked over to the fridge in the kitchen and effortlessly lifted it up with one hand, surprising the Thompsons. "I have the strength of a gorilla, one of the many abilities that Animalians can possess."

Amanda and John were amazed by what they just saw, but still uncertain. Mr. Black then offered some materials about the Sanctuary, including books and flyers, to read and learn more about the school.

Mr. Black spoke up, addressing Ethan's parents with a reassuring tone. "I understand your skepticism. It's only natural to be wary of the unknown. But I urge you to come and see for yourselves what the Sanctuary is all about. The first day of school is just a few months away, and it would give you a glimpse into this world that may seem strange to you now. Trust me, it will be worth your while."

Ethan chimed in, eager for his parents to allow him to explore the wonders of the Animalian world. "Please, Mom, Dad. I really think we should come and check it out. What's the worst that can happen?"

John, Ethan's father, let out a sigh and reluctantly agreed. "Alright, we'll come. But I have to admit, this whole thing still sounds a bit crazy to me." He let out a chuckle and added, "I just hope I don't end up turning into a cat or something."

CHAPTER 3

THE TIME IN BETWEEN

Ethan was counting down the days until the start of classes at the Sanctuary. Although the current school year was near the end, he would need to wait through the whole summer before going to his new school. He had spent the last few days reading through the books that Mr. Black had given him, trying to learn as much as he could about the Animalian world. He was fascinated by the stories of different people with special abilities, and he couldn't wait to learn more.

He had also been trying to find more information online, but he quickly realized that there was very little to be found beyond shady conspiracy websites. The Animalian world was shrouded in secrecy, and it seemed that most of the information was only available to those who were a part of it.

He learned about the different animal talents that existed among the Animalians, and the various classes that the Sanctuary offered to help them hone and control their abilities. He read about the famous Animalian artist, Jessica Hawks, a bird-powered singer who was known for her stunning voice, and the renowned Animalian chef, Liam Chen, who could control the flavors of food with his bee-like abilities and create delicious desserts.

He also learned about classes such as "Feline Agility and Stealth" and "Canine Tracking and Scent," which were specifically designed to help Animalians with those specific talents. As he read, he felt excited about the opportunities that awaited him at the Sanctuary. He couldn't wait to start learning and training, and to finally find his place among his own kind.

❖

Ethan sat nervously at his desk, counting down the minutes until the final bell of the school year ring. He had been eagerly awaiting the day when he could finally leave this place and start his new life at the Sanctuary. As the final bell rang, Ethan gathered his things and started to make his way to the bus stop. He had been dreading this moment all day, knowing that his bullies would be waiting for him. He had managed to avoid them for the most part during the school year, but he knew they would be looking for a final chance to torment him before the summer break.

Sure enough, as he walked down the sidewalk, he heard their jeering voices behind him. "Hey, look who it is, the little weirdo!" Brad shouted. "Where you going, freak? You think you're too good for us now?"

Ethan quickened his pace, but the bullies were closing in. He could hear their laughter and taunts getting louder and more aggressive. He knew he couldn't outrun them, so he made a split-second decision and headed towards the street where cars were driving by.

To his surprise, he leaped over the incoming van with ease, leaving the bullies behind, shocked and bewildered. Ethan landed on the other side and kept running, not looking back until he was sure he had lost them. He couldn't believe what had just happened, he had never been athletic and jumping that high should have been impossible. He realized that he had used his powers for the first time, and a wave of excitement and fear took over him.

Ethan couldn't believe what had just happened. He had easily outrun and outmaneuvered his bullies, leaping effortlessly over the van to escape them. He didn't want to ride the bus no more and as he ran home, he felt a sense of lightness and power in each step. The fear he had felt moments before had turned into excitement as he began to realize the potential of his abilities.

He remembered the way he had felt on the playground, the urge to fly and escape his problems. He had always been fascinated by birds, and now he understood why. He had always felt different, disconnected from the world around him, but now it all made sense. He was different because he was special. He had special abilities, and he couldn't wait to explore them.

Getting home, Ethan didn't skip a beat, he grabbed his camera and went outside again. He couldn't stop smiling as he ran through the streets, camera in hand. He felt like he was flying, his feet barely touching the ground as he ran. He had never felt so light and free before. He knew that his capabilities were starting to manifest, and he looked forward to see what else he was capable of.

As he ran, he noticed how effortlessly he was able to take pictures. He had always been good at photography, but now it seemed like he had some sort of falcon-like ability to focus and target. He could spot a bird flying high in the sky and zoom in, capturing it in perfect detail. He could see a leaf on a tree from a block away and adjust his lens to get the perfect shot. He felt like he had some sort of special connection to the world around him, and it was exhilarating.

He spent the rest of the day running and taking pictures, exploring the city and seeing it in a whole new way. He felt like he was seeing things for the first time, and he couldn't wait to start his new life as an Animalian.

The summer break was a blur for Ethan. He spent most of his days reading the books that Mr. Black had given him, learning all he could about the Animalian world and the Sanctuary. He also spent a lot of time running. He found that he was faster and more agile than he had ever been before, and he loved the feeling of the wind in his hair and the sun on his face as he sprinted through the streets. He felt free and alive, and he knew that his abilities were starting to manifest.

He also took a lot of pictures. His passion for photography had only grown stronger, and he found that he was able to capture stunning images even while on the move. He would run through the city, camera in hand, chasing after birds and other animals, trying to capture the perfect shot.

As the day approached, Ethan began to worry about the practicalities of attending a school for Animalians. He didn't know what to pack, and he wasn't sure if he should bring any of his favorite things from home. He wondered if he should take his pet toy with him, a stuffed falcon he had had since he was a child, but he wasn't sure if that would be offensive to the other Animalians. He felt silly thinking about it but there was so much of this world he didn't know.

As the summer break came to an end, Ethan couldn't wait to start classes at the Sanctuary. He hoped that the other Animalians would be nothing like the bullies at his school. He longed to connect with people who understood what it was like to feel different.

CHAPTER 4

JOURNEY TO THE SANCTUARY

❖

Ethan was nervous as he stepped off the plane with his parents. He had read all of the books that Mr. Black had given him, but he still wasn't sure what to expect. He scanned the airport for any sign of the bus stop that would take him to the Sanctuary, but he didn't know what he was looking for. Should he look for a bus stop that had people with fur and feathers? None of the books had mentioned any significant physical differences between Animalians and humans, but Ethan wouldn't be surprised if there were some. He felt a small flutter of excitement in his chest as he wondered what kind of people he would meet at the Sanctuary. As they walked through the airport, Ethan's parents chatted excitedly about the trip and the Sanctuary, but Ethan was too focused on looking for the bus stop to pay much attention.

The air was crisp and fresh, and the scent of pine trees filled the air. Ethan couldn't believe that this was where the Sanctuary was located. It seemed like such a peaceful and idyllic place, far removed from the hustle and bustle of the city.

Ethan and his parents finally found the bus stop for the Sanctuary chartered bus, it had the distinct Sanctuary emblem on it, a shield featuring a lion in the center surrounded by other animals. As they approached, Ethan couldn't help but feel a mix of excitement and anxiety. As he looked around, he was surprised to see that everyone looked normal. They were all dressed in normal clothes, and there was nothing about them that set them apart from the average person. Ethan felt a little disappointed, but he knew that appearances could be deceiving. He had read in the books that Animalians could conceal their abilities, so he decided to keep an open mind.

As they waited for the bus to arrive, Ethan looked around at the other people waiting. There were a few families with children, a couple of older people, and a group of teenagers that looked around his age. He wondered if they were all Animalians like him. He was so lost in his thoughts that he didn't notice when the bus arrived until his parents called him over. They climbed aboard and found their seats.

As he took his seat, he noticed a girl sitting next to him. She had dark curly hair and brown eyes, and she was fidgeting with her backpack. "Hi," Ethan said, trying to make conversation. "I'm Ethan."

The girl smiled. "Hi, I'm Emma," she said. "I've never seen you before, are you new to the Sanctuary?"

"Yeah, it will be my first year there," Ethan replied.

"That's awesome," Emma said, her eyes lighting up. "I've been attending the Sanctuary for a couple years now. It's a great place to learn how to control our abilities. And the people there are amazing too. You'll love it."

"Sounds exciting. So, what kind of Animalian are you?" he asked.

"I'm a bear Animalian," Emma replied. "My body have the strength and endurance of a bear. It's pretty cool, but it's also a lot to handle."

Ethan nodded, understanding the weight of her words. Emma turned to Ethan and asked, "Have you always known you were an Animalian? I've known since I was a kid, but my parents are both Animalians so it wasn't a surprise."

Ethan shook his head, "No, I only found out recently. A man named Mr. Black, he's a gorilla Animalian, told me about the Sanctuary and convinced my parents to let me come here."

Emma's eyes widened in surprise, "Wow, that's really cool. I know Mr. Black, he is one of my favorite teachers. So, what kind of Animalian are you? What's your power?"

Ethan hesitated, unsure of how to answer. He didn't even know what his abilities were yet, he had only had a glimpse of it when chased by his bullies. "I'm not really sure," he admitted, "I haven't really had a chance to figure it out yet."

Emma nodded, "Oh, that's interesting. Any idea or hint about where your talents may be?"

Ethan shook his head, "No, I have no idea. I mean... I just know that when I run, it feels like I'm flying and I have a strong connection to birds."

Emma smiled, "Well, it sounds like you might have an avian spirit."

Ethan was intrigued, "Really? Tell me more about this spirit thing."

Emma went on to explain, "Well, it's not something that's necessarily proven, but many Animalians believe that our powers come from the spirits of animals that live in coexistence with our human spirit. It's a way for us to connect with our animalistic side and tap into our primal instincts. Some people even believe that each Animalian has a specific animal spirit that guides them and helps them access their abilities. It's a fascinating concept."

Ethan listened intently, feeling a sense of understanding. He had always felt different and disconnected from the world around him, but this concept of animal spirits made sense to him. He felt a connection to birds, and the idea that his powers might come from a bird spirit was exciting to him.

"Wow, that's really cool," Ethan said, "I've never heard of anything like that before. It's like discovering a whole new world."

Emma nodded thoughtfully. "Yeah, there are different theories about where our talents come from. Some people believe in the spirit animal theory, but others think it's more of a biological thing, like a genetic mutation or something like that. I'm not sure which one I believe in, but I do know that I've always had this connection to bears. Even as a kid, I always felt drawn to them, and now that I have these powers, it makes sense."

Emma's eyes caught the glimpse of a camera peeking out from the top of Ethan's backpack. "Is that a camera?" she asked, leaning forward in her seat to get a better look.

Ethan smiled, "Yeah, I'm into photography. I like to capture the beauty of nature and birds."

Emma's eyes lit up, "That's so cool! Can I see some of your photos?"

Ethan nodded and reached for his camera, pulling it out of his backpack. He flipped through the photos, showing Emma some of his favorites. She was impressed by the quality and the composition of the shots.

"These are amazing, Ethan," Emma said. "You have a real talent for photography."

Ethan blushed, feeling a sense of pride. He had always loved photography, and it was nice to have someone appreciate his work.

"Thanks," he said. "I've always been fascinated how light and color can tell a story. I feel like photography is a way to express myself and connect with the world around me."

Emma nodded, "I can definitely see that in your photos. They're very evocative and emotional."

As they continued to talk and look at Ethan's photos, the bus ride passed quickly. Before they knew it, they had arrived at the Sanctuary. As they gathered their things and prepared to disembark, Emma turned to Ethan.

"I'm really looking forward to getting to know you better, Ethan," she said. "I think we're going to have a lot in common."

Ethan smiled, feeling excited. He had never felt like he fit in with the other kids at school, but he had a feeling that things were about to change.

As they stepped off the bus and looked around at the sprawling campus, Ethan knew that he was finally where he belonged.

The Sanctuary was a grand, sprawling campus that was nestled in the heart of the mountains. The main building was a large, imposing structure that was made of natural stone and wood, with large windows that let in ample natural light. The building was surrounded by lush gardens and greenery, with well-manicured lawns and a beautiful pond that was home to a variety of different species of birds. The Sanctuary was designed to blend seamlessly into its natural surroundings, with the architecture and landscaping reflecting the beauty of the surrounding nature.

The campus was home to several different buildings, including dormitories, classrooms, and research facilities. The dormitories were spacious and comfortable, with each room being shared by two students. The classrooms were well-equipped, with the latest technology and resources for teaching. The research facilities were state-of-the-art, and were used for studying Animalian powers, genetics, and other related topics.

The Sanctuary also had several recreational facilities, including a gym, a swimming pool, and a library. The gym was equipped with the latest exercise equipment, and was used for training and developing Animalian powers. The swimming pool was a perfect place to relax and cool off after a workout. The library was a great place to study and research, and it had a wide variety of books and resources on Animalian powers and related topics.

A young man with a big smile on his face greeted them. "Welcome to the Sanctuary!" he exclaimed, "I'm Doug, and I'll be your guide for today. You are the Thompson family."

Ethan's parents looked at each other in confusion, "How do you know who we are?" asked Ethan's father.

"Well, you smell just like Mr. Black did when he came back after meeting you," he said with a chuckle. "Don't worry, it's a good thing. My sense of smell is incredibly heightened, it's one of my dog-like powers. Not creepy at all."

"Nice to meet you, Doug," Ethan said, extending his hand.

Doug shook it firmly, Ethan's parents smiled nervously, still not quite sure what to make of the whole Animalian thing.

"Come on, I'll give you a tour of the place," Doug said, leading them towards the main building.

As they walked, Doug pointed out different buildings and facilities, explaining what they were for. "This is the main building, where you'll find classrooms, the library, and the cafeteria. Over there is the dormitory, where you'll be staying. And over there," he said, pointing to a large field, "is where we have sports and training exercises."

Ethan's parents asked several questions, and Doug answered them patiently. He showed them the different classrooms, the library, and the cafeteria. He also introduced them to some of the teachers and staff.

As they walked through the dormitory, Doug explained the rules and regulations of the Sanctuary. He also showed them the room where Ethan would be staying, and helped them unpack.

Ethan's parents were impressed by the Sanctuary, and they could see how excited their son was about the whole thing. They were still a bit nervous about leaving their child here, but they knew that this was the best place for him.

Doug, noticing their worries, assured them that Ethan would be safe and well taken care of at the Sanctuary. He also gave them his contact information, and told them that they could reach him anytime if they needed anything.

Ethan's parents thanked Doug for his kindness, and they all said their goodbyes. As they left, Ethan felt a sense of excitement and anticipation for what was to come at the Sanctuary. He couldn't wait to start learning about his powers, and to meet other Animalians like himself.

Ethan was just settling up in his room when he heard someone enter. He turned around to see his new roommate, a skinny black boy with a big smile on his face. The boy introduced himself as Marcus and Ethan did the same.

"Nice to meet you, Ethan," Marcus said, extending his hand.

Ethan shook his hand and smiled. "Nice to meet you too, Marcus."

"So, what's your animal spirit?" Marcus asked, his curiosity getting the better of him.

Ethan hesitated for a moment, unsure of how to answer. "I'm not really sure yet," he said. "I've had some strange experiences lately, but I haven't been able to figure out what my animal or my powers are."

"I know what you mean," Marcus said, nodding. "I'm an owl. I have a sharp mind and the ability to see things from... let's say different perspectives. I can also stay up late, but don't worry, I won't be hooting in the middle of the night," he said with a grin.

Ethan smiled, "That's cool, I've never heard of an owl Animalian before."

Marcus nodded, "Yeah, we're not exactly common. But I think it's a good thing, it makes us unique and special."

Ethan nodded, "So, how long have you been coming to the Sanctuary?" he asked.

"I've been here for two years, starting my third year now," Marcus replied. "It's been a great experience, I've learned so much and I've met so many amazing people."

"That sounds great," Ethan said, sounding envious. "I hope I can have a similar experience here."

Marcus nodded, "You will. Just give it time and embrace your powers, you'll see how amazing it can be."

CHAPTER 5

A NEW ERA OF LEARNING

The next morning, Ethan and Marcus met up in the dormitory hall and made their way to the assembly hall together. As they walked, they couldn't help but notice the diverse group of students around them. Some had slightly pointed ears or a slight slant to their eyes, subtle hints at their animal spirits. Others had more obvious features, like a dusting of freckles across their nose that looked eerily like spots.

As they walked, they saw Emma sitting alone at a bench, looking at a map of the Sanctuary. They approached her and greeted her. Emma smiled and greeted them back, and they continued walking together.

"Hey guys!" she greeted them with a smile. "I was wondering if we were going to run into each other again."

Ethan and Marcus exchanged a quick glance before smiling back at her. "Yeah, it's great to see you again," Ethan said.

Ethan noticed that the Sanctuary was much larger than he had imagined. The buildings were grand and imposing, with tall columns and intricate carvings. The gardens were lush and well-maintained, with paths winding through them.

As they entered the auditorium, Ethan saw that the stage was set up with a podium and a large banner that read "Welcome to the Sanctuary". Students were filing into the seats, chatting excitedly with one another. Ethan, Marcus, and Emma found seats towards the middle of the auditorium.

After a few minutes, a hush fell over the crowd as the headmaster of the Sanctuary, Leo Braveheart, walked onto the stage. He had a thick head of salt-and-pepper hair, which he kept well-groomed and styled in a neat cut. He also had a well-trimmed beard and mustache, which gave him a distinguished and regal look. His face was chiseled and strong, with high cheekbones and a strong jawline. He had piercing blue eyes, and a deep, commanding voice that could fill a room. He carried himself with an air of authority and confidence, and it was clear that he was a leader. He dressed in a simple, yet elegant, suit, and a golden lion pin was fastened to his lapel. Braveheart began with his deep voice:

"Welcome to the Sanctuary! For many of you, this may be your first time here, and for others, it may be a familiar home. Regardless, we are all united in our purpose: to learn and to grow as Animalians.

As you may know, Animalians have existed among humans for centuries, but it is only in recent times that we have been able to gather and educate ourselves in a safe and accepting environment. Here, at the Sanctuary, you will have the opportunity to learn about your powers, hone your skills, and discover your place in the world.

You will learn from some of the most accomplished and knowledgeable Animalians in the world. You will have access to state-of-the-art facilities and equipment. And you will be surrounded by a community of individuals who understand and accept you for who you are.

But the Sanctuary is not just about learning, it's also about discovery. It's about embracing who you are and what you are capable of. It's about understanding your place in the world, and learning how to use your abilities to make a positive impact on society.

As headmaster, I promise to guide and support you throughout your journey here at the Sanctuary. I encourage you to take advantage of all the opportunities that are presented to you, and to always strive to be the best versions of yourselves.

So, welcome once again to the Sanctuary. Let's begin this journey together and discover what we are truly capable of."

Ethan was surprised to learn that he would still have to take normal human subjects like math, English, and science, but he was even more excited about the Animalian classes that were offered at the Sanctuary. He couldn't wait to learn about Animalian history, and how the different Animalian communities interacted with each other and with humans throughout history. He was also excited about the class on Animalian powers, where he would learn about the different talents that Animalians possessed, and how to control and use his own abilities. Other classes he was looking forward to were "Animal in the wild" where he would learn about the different animals and their behavior, and "Animal Mythology" where he would learn about the different animals and their symbolism in different cultures. Overall, Ethan was excited to learn more about his own heritage and the world of Animalians.

Ethan, Marcus, and Emma were sitting in the courtyard during lunch, discussing their upcoming class schedule for the day. "I can't wait for Animalian History," Emma said excitedly.

"Me neither," Marcus added. "I've heard that the teacher is really old, like over 100 years old."

Ethan raised an eyebrow. "Really? How is that possible?"

Emma shrugged. "It's probably because of his animal spirit. I heard he's a tortoise."

"Wow," Ethan said in amazement. "I wonder what other secrets we'll learn in that class."

Marcus laughed. "I hope we'll learn how to live forever, then we'll never have to worry about getting old."

The three friends chuckled, finishing their lunch and getting ready to head to their next class. "Come on," Emma said, standing up. "Let's go meet Mr. Smith and learn some cool stuff."

The three of them headed off towards the classroom, chatting excitedly about the possibilities of what they might learn in Animalian History.

They walked into the class. The room was dimly lit, with only a few flickering candles on the desks providing any light. The walls were adorned with tapestries depicting ancient Animalian battles and symbols. In the center of the room stood a large wooden desk, behind which sat Mr. Smith. He was an old man, with a bald head and wrinkled skin. He had a stern expression on his face, but his eyes sparkled with intelligence and wisdom.

As the three students took their seats, Mr. Smith began to speak. "Welcome, young Animalians," he said in a deep, gravelly voice. "I am George Smith, and I will be your guide on a journey through the rich and fascinating history of our kind. Today, we will begin by exploring the ancient origins of the Animalian race, and the myths and legends that have shaped our understanding of the world."

Ethan was intrigued by the topic and couldn't wait to learn more about Animalian history. He noticed that Marcus was also paying attention and Emma was taking notes. They were all eager to learn more about the past of the Animalian race and the secrets that it held.

Mr. Smith continued his lecture, talking about the different theories of how the Animalian race came to be, and the different legends that had been passed down through the generations. Ethan listened intently, taking in every word. He was fascinated by the stories of powerful Animalian leaders who had risen to power in the past, and the great battles that had shaped the course of history.

As the class of Animalian History came to an end and the other students began to file out of the classroom, Ethan hung back. He approached Mr. Smith, who was gathering his papers and putting them away in his briefcase.

"Mr. Smith," Ethan began, "I was wondering if I could talk to you for a moment."

"Of course, Ethan," Mr. Smith replied, his wise eyes crinkling at the corners. "What's on your mind?"

"Well," Ethan hesitated, "I haven't been able to unlock my abilities yet. I'm not sure how to do it."

"Ah, the age-old question," Mr. Smith said with a smile. "Unlocking your powers is a journey, Ethan. It's not something that can be rushed or forced. It takes time and patience. You must first understand and accept your animal spirit."

Ethan nodded, taking in Mr. Smith's words.

"It's important to remember that our talents come from a deep connection with our animal spirit. It's not just about physical strength or abilities, but also about understanding the spirit's wisdom and way of life. Spend time in nature, meditate, and try to understand the characteristics and behavior of your animal spirit. It will help you to connect with it and unlock your powers," Mr. Smith explained.

"Thank you, Mr. Smith," Ethan said, feeling a sense of calm. "I'll definitely try that."

"Good luck on your journey, Ethan," Mr. Smith said with a smile. "And remember, don't be in a rush, enjoy the process."

As Ethan and Mr. Smith finished their conversation, the older man let out a deep sigh and turned towards the door. "I have another class in an hour," he said, "and if I don't start walking now, I'll be late."

Ethan inevitably chuckled as he watched the old man make his way towards the door. Mr. Smith walked at an extremely slow pace, as if he was in no hurry to get anywhere. Each step was deliberate and measured, savoring each movement. Ethan couldn't believe how slow he was moving, it was as if he was in slow motion. After what felt like many minutes later the old man said "Well, I suppose I'll see you in class," finally reaching the door. "Try not to be late," he added with a twinkle in his eye, and with that, he was gone.

Ethan couldn't help but laugh, as he shook his head and made his way out of the classroom. He knew that he would never forget Mr. Smith's words or the way he walked, it was just too funny.

CHAPTER 6

RISING TO THE CHALLENGE

Ethan woke up early. It was the second day of classes at the Sanctuary. As he was getting dressed, he noticed that Marcus was asleep, snoring softly. He shook him gently, trying to wake him up. "Come on, Marcus. We don't want to be late for Animal in Motion class," Ethan said.

Marcus groaned, rubbing his eyes. "Ugh, I hate mornings," he grumbled. "But I guess it's better than sleeping all night. As an owl, I don't sleep at night, but I do need a few naps during the day. And man, early morning sunlight is the worst!"

Ethan and Marcus quickly got ready and headed to the class. Animal in Motion was a class designed to help students unlock and control their powers through physical activities and exercises. The class was held in a large gymnasium, with various obstacles and equipment set up to challenge the students.

As they walked into the gym, Ethan saw a group of students stretching and warming up. He recognized Emma among them and gave her a wave. Emma smiled and waved back.

The class began with a series of warm-up exercises and stretches, led by a teacher named Ms. Park. She was a tall and lean woman, with long black hair that she often kept pulled back into a ponytail. She had sharp, angular features and a determined look in her dark brown eyes. She was of Asian descent and was known for her fierce and tenacious attitude, much like the spirit animal she inherited her powers from, the horse. She was a natural athlete and always pushed her students to be the best that they can be. Despite her tough exterior, she cared deeply for her students and was always willing to help them unlock their full potential.

After the warm-up, Ms. Park divided the students into small groups and assigned them different stations, each one designed to challenge a specific aspect of their powers. Ethan found himself at a station with Marcus and Emma, where they were tasked with jumping over and dodging obstacles while trying to maintain their balance.

The class was a combination of physical exercise and animal-inspired movements. Ethan and Emma found it easy to keep up with the exercises, their bodies responding naturally to the movements. Marcus, on the other hand, was struggling to keep up. He was not a natural athlete and found the class challenging.

The Stone brothers were three mischievous young men with Latino heritage and coyote spirits. The triplets had dark brown hair and eyes, and lean builds. They were called Jake, Tyler and Zack. They were always joking around and playing pranks, but they had a tendency to take it too far.

As soon as they saw Marcus, they started to laugh and mock him. Marcus tried to ignore them, but they continued to taunt him. Ethan and Emma noticed what was happening and decided to step up to defend their friend. "Leave him alone," said Ethan, trying to be brave. "Yeah, why don't you pick on someone your own size," added Emma.

The Stone brothers didn't like being confronted and decided to take it out on Emma. Jake stepped forward and pushed her. To everyone's surprise, Emma easily and effortlessly pushed him back with her bear strength. Jake stumbled and fell to the floor. "What was that?" asked Tyler, surprised. Emma stood tall and looked at the triplets with a fierce determination. "I am not someone you want to mess with," she said confidently.

Ms. Park, who had been watching the situation, walked over to the group. "Is there a problem here?" she asked. Emma explained what had happened and how the Stone brothers had been provoking Marcus. Ms. Park looked at the triplets with disapproval. "That kind of behavior is not tolerated here at the Sanctuary," she said firmly. "I suggest you apologize and make amends."

The Stone brothers apologized. From then on, they left Marcus and the group alone, and focused on their studies. Emma became known as the "bear" of the group, and was respected and admired by her peers for standing up for what was right.

Ethan's heart was pounding as he approached the obstacle in front of him. It was a large hurdle, about twice his height, and he could feel the adrenaline running through his veins. It wasn't part of the normal obstacle course but he wanted to give it a try. He took a deep breath and focused on the task at hand.

As he began to run, he felt a sense of weightlessness surge through him. His feet barely seemed to touch the ground and he felt as if he were gliding rather than running. He could feel the wind in his hair and the sun on his face as he approached the hurdle.

With a powerful leap, he sailed over the obstacle, feeling as if he were flying. For a brief moment, he felt truly free and alive. But then, reality hit him and he realized that he was falling. He tumbled to the ground, the wind knocked out of him.

As he lay there, catching his breath, he could not avoid the feeling of disappointment that was engulfing him. He had tasted what it was like to truly fly and now it was gone.

Emma rushed over to him, concern etched on her face. "Are you okay? Are you hurt?" she asked as she helped him to his feet.

Ethan shook his head, still trying to process what had just happened. "I...I don't know. I felt like I was flying for a second, but then I fell."

The Stone brothers laughed, "Looks like someone needs to stick to running," one of them jeered.

But Emma wasn't having it. "Hey, leave him alone," she said, shooting them a glare. "Ethan, don't listen to them. You did great. You're going to get the hang of it, I know it." She grinned at him, trying to lighten the mood. "Besides, you're not the only one who's fallen today. Jake here took a pretty nasty spill during training a few minutes ago," she said, nodding towards one of the Stone brothers.

Ethan couldn't resist chuckling at the thought of one of the Stone brothers falling on their face. It was a small victory, but it made him feel better. "Thanks, Emma," he said, smiling at her gratefully.

Ethan felt a sense of determination as he got back up on his feet. He dusted himself off and looked at the obstacle in front of him. It was a large hurdle that he was supposed to jump over, but the fall earlier had shaken his confidence.

He took a deep breath and focused all his energy on the task at hand. He started running towards the hurdle, picking up speed with each step. As he approached the obstacle, he leaped into the air, his body soaring over the barrier. For a moment, it felt like he was flying. He landed on his feet on the other side of the hurdle, and the class erupted into cheers.

Emma rushed over to him and gave him a big hug, covering his face with her curly hair. "You did it!" she exclaimed.

"I can't believe it," Ethan said, still in shock.

Marcus and the rest of the class came over to give Ethan high fives and congratulations. Even Ms. Park gave him a pat on the back and a smile.

"Great job, Ethan," she said. "You've unlocked a new level of your abilities. Keep pushing yourself, and you'll be surprised at what you can achieve."

Ethan couldn't stop smiling, feeling prideful on his accomplishment. But he knew that this was just the beginning of his journey to unlocking his full potential.

After classes in the afternoon, Ethan had some free time and decided to take advantage of the beautiful scenery the

Sanctuary had to offer. He grabbed his camera and went around the property, taking pictures of the lush gardens, the pond, and the towering trees. He invited Marcus to come with him, but his roommate declined, saying he was going to take a nap and catch up on some reading. Ethan didn't mind, he was excited to explore and capture the beauty of the Sanctuary through his camera lens. He walked around for a while, snapping pictures and admiring the natural beauty of the place. He even stumbled upon some of the animal inhabitants of the Sanctuary and snapped some pictures of them too. He felt a sense of peace and serenity being surrounded by nature, and it made him forget about his struggles for a little while.

As he walked, he came across a group of students practicing their animal powers on the sports field. One of them, a young man with the spirit of a cheetah, was sprinting at incredible speeds around a track while another, a purple hair girl with the spirit of a hummingbird, was dancing high in the sky. Ethan was awestruck as he watched them, snapping pictures of their impressive feats from afar.

As he continued his tour, he came across a group of staff members discussing some plans for a new project. Seeing Ethan with the camera on hand, one of them joked, "Just make sure you don't feed these images to any conspiracy websites."

Ethan laughed, "Don't worry, I'm just here to document the beauty of the Sanctuary."

The staff members smiled and went back to their discussion as Ethan continued on his photography tour, capturing the unique and diverse beauty around him.

Ethan also came across a large library, which was home to countless books and manuscripts. The library was full of people of all ages, reading, studying and discussing. He snapped a few photos of the library and its patrons, capturing the intellectual spirit of the Sanctuary.

Lastly, he came across a large lake and took some photos of the sunset reflecting in the water. The lake was bordered by a walking path and some benches where residents were enjoying the view. It was home to different species of birds and fish, some of them trained by the Animalian residents.

Ethan was lost in thought, he was so focused on capturing the perfect shot that he didn't even notice Emma sneaking up behind him. Suddenly, she jumped out and shouted, "Boo!"

Ethan jumped and let out a small yelp, but quickly laughed it off. "You scared me," he said, still laughing.

"Sorry, I couldn't resist," Emma said, grinning.

They sat down on a nearby bench, and she asked him about his photography. Ethan showed her some of the pictures he had taken and explained how he was trying to capture the beauty and diversity of the Sanctuary.

"It's amazing," Emma said, looking at the photos. "You really have a talent for this."

"Thanks," Ethan said, feeling proud.

"So, what classes are you liking the most so far?" She asked.

"Well, I'm really enjoying the Animalian Technology class. It's so cool to learn about all the ways we can use technology to enhance our abilities," Ethan said.

"Eh, that class is so boring. I'd rather be in the Animalian Mythology class, learning about all the crazy stories and legends," Emma said, rolling her eyes.

"Mythology? More like myth-o-logy," Ethan said, chuckling.

"Ha ha, very funny," Emma said, playfully punching his arm. "I know, I know. But seriously, it's important to understand our past and the stories that have shaped us as Animalians," Emma said.

"I guess you have a point," Ethan said, shrugging.

"But enough about classes, let's talk about something more interesting. Like, have you ever tried to fly?" Emma asked, wiggling her eyebrows.

"Fly? Like, with wings? That's impossible," Ethan said, laughing.

"Hey, anything is possible with our abilities. I bet you could fly if you really tried," Emma said, with a grin.

"Yeah, right. I'll stick to taking photos for now," Ethan said, snapping a picture of Emma making a silly face.

"Hey, delete that!" Emma said, trying to grab the camera.

Ethan laughed and dodged her grab, "It's too late, it's already on the internet."

"Ugh, you're impossible," Emma said, laughing and shaking her head.

CHAPTER 7

ANIMAL COMMUNICATION

❖

The classroom for the new class called "Animal Communication" was unlike any other Ethan had been in. Instead of the usual desks and chairs, there were perches and little beds spread throughout the room, each housing a different type of animal. There were parrots, owls, snakes, and even a baby elephant in the corner. There was a majestic falcon perched on a stand in the corner, its piercing gaze seeming to take in the entire room. Across the room, a family of foxes huddled together in a large pen, their bushy tails twitching with curiosity as they took in the newcomers. Ms.

Rodriguez, a tall, slender woman with long, dark hair, stood at the front of the room with her parrot companion perched on her shoulder.

As the students filed in, Ethan felt a little overwhelmed. He had never been around so many animals at once, let alone trying to communicate with them. He took a seat next to Emma and Marcus, who seemed just as excited as he was about this new class.

"Welcome, students," said Ms. Rodriguez, her parrot squawking in agreement. "I know some of you may be nervous about this class, but I assure you, it's nothing to be afraid of. We are all here to learn and grow together."

Ethan couldn't help but feel a pang of worry. He had no idea how he was going to communicate with these animals. He didn't even know what his animal spirit was yet, but he was determined to give it his best shot.

"For those of you who already know your animal spirit, I encourage you to find the corresponding animal in the room and begin to establish a connection. For those of you who are still unsure, or if your animal spirit is not represented here, find an animal that you feel a connection with and begin to establish communication. And remember, communication is a two-way street. Not only should you be listening for their thoughts, but also projecting your own."

As she spoke, the parrot perched on her shoulder squawked excitedly, as if eager to join in on the lesson. "And as my assistant, Polly, likes to remind me, it's important to remember that animals have their own personalities and ways of communicating. It may take some time to establish a connection and understand what they are trying to convey."

Ethan walked around the classroom, looking at the various animals that were there. Some of his classmates were already interacting with their corresponding animals, like Marcus with his owl. He noticed a small group of mice in one corner, and a group of birds, including a parrot, in another. He felt a pull towards the birds, but he couldn't quite put his finger on why.

As he walked closer, he saw a falcon sitting on a perch, its head turning to look at him as he approached. He could feel a strange connection to the bird, and as he looked into its eyes, he felt like he was seeing a piece of himself reflected back at him. He reached out a hand tentatively, and the falcon leaned its head down to nuzzle his palm.

Ethan felt a sense of understanding and familiarity flood over him, like he had known this bird for his whole life. He had a sudden urge to communicate with it, to tell it everything that was on his mind. He closed his eyes and focused on the falcon, and to his surprise, he found that he could sense what it was thinking and feeling. The falcon was content and peaceful, and it seemed to be looking forward to flying around the Sanctuary.

Ethan opened his eyes and looked at the falcon in amazement. "We have the same animal spirit," he whispered. The falcon seemed to nod in agreement, and Ethan felt a wave of joy and excitement. And then, as if a lightbulb had turned on in his head, Ethan knew the falcon's name. "Talon," he whispered. The falcon cocked its head to one side, as if in agreement. Ethan grinned, feeling excitement and connection to this animal he had just met.

Ms. Rodriguez, who had been observing Ethan's interaction with the falcon, smiled. "It looks like you've made a connection," she said. "Talon, is it?"

Ethan nodded, still in awe of what had just happened. "Yes, his name is Talon."

The rest of the class passed by in a blur as Ethan spent the rest of the time talking to Talon and learning more about the bird and its habits. The bell rang and the students began to gather their things and head for the door. One boy, in particular, rushed towards the exit, limping heavily on one leg. He seemed to be in a hurry. Ethan approached his new companion, Talon, who was perched on a perch in the corner of the classroom.

"See you later Talon," Ethan said, smiling at the falcon.

"I'll be looking forward to it," Talon replied, or at least that's what Ethan felt he said.

As he walked, he noticed from the corner of his eye a commotion happening on the other side of the room. Curious, he turned his head to see what was going on and was shocked to see a small baby elephant that had fainted. The other students around the elephant were panicking and trying to revive it, while the teacher, Ms. Rodriguez, was rushing over to assess the situation.

"What happened here?" Ms. Rodriguez asked, her parrot companion squawking in alarm.

"I don't know," a student named Michael said, a look of concern etched on his face. "One moment he was fine, munching on hay, and then he just fell over."

Ethan approached the elephant, noticing that its breathing was shallow and labored. He felt a pang of guilt, wishing he had paid more attention to other animals during class.

"We need to call for help," Ms. Rodriguez said urgently. "Someone call the vet."

Ethan watched as the vet rushed in, quickly examining the elephant and administering some medication. The animal's breathing became less labored.

"He's going to be okay," the vet reassured them, "but we need to keep a close eye on him for the next days."

Ethan walked into his dorm room, his backpack slung over his shoulder. "Hey Marcus, what's up?"

Marcus, who was sitting at his desk with his back to Ethan, turned his head 180 degrees to face him. "Not much, just reading up on some owl facts."

Ethan shuddered. "Dude, stop doing that. It creeps me out."

Marcus laughed. "Sorry, I can't help it. It's just a handy owl power. So, what's up with you?"

Ethan tossed his backpack onto his bed and plopped down next to it. "Nothing much, just trying to figure out what classes I want to focus on. How about you? What classes are you into?"

Marcus leaned back in his chair, considering. "I'm really interested in the classes that focus on the animal side of things, like Animalian History and Communicating with Animals. But I also want to make sure I don't fall behind in the normal human classes."

Ethan nodded. "Yeah, I know what you mean. I'm trying to balance it all too. But I'm really excited for the Animal In Motion class. I think it'll help me unlock my powers."

"Yeah, that class is pretty intense," Marcus said with a chuckle. "But I'm sure you'll do great. You're a natural athlete."

Ethan grinned. "Thanks man. I'm just excited to see what I can do. So, what are you reading about now?"

Marcus turned back to his book. "Did you know that some owls can turn their heads almost all the way around?"

Ethan rolled his eyes. "Yeah, I know. And it's still creepy."

"Dude, you won't believe what I learned in mythology class today," Marcus exclaimed. "There's this thing called a Dragon Animalian, and they're supposed to be super powerful. Like, they can fly and control fire and all kinds of crazy stuff." He leaned forward in excitement, "I mean, can you imagine? Being able to fly and breathe fire? That would be so cool!"

Ethan's eyes widened at the mention of the Dragon Animalians. Maybe mythology classes wasn't as boring as he thought it was. "No way, seriously? I've never heard of those before," he exclaimed.

"Yeah, it's pretty cool. Apparently they were really rare and all of them are believed to be extinct now," Marcus replied.

"It would be so cool to have that power," Ethan said, thinking out loud.

"Yeah, but it also comes with a lot of responsibility. You have to be able to control it and not use it recklessly," Marcus added.

"I know, I know. It's just a cool thought," Ethan chuckled.

"Well, I wouldn't get too excited about it. The chances of you being a Dragon Animalian are pretty slim," Marcus said with a smirk.

Ethan rolled his eyes playfully. "Thanks for the encouragement, Marcus. Hey, have you heard anything about the baby elephant that fainted in class today?"

"Oh, Elmer? Yeah, I heard he's still unconscious and it looks like he was poisoned," Marcus replied, closing his book. "It's really sad, I hope he's okay."

Ethan furrowed his brows in confusion. "Elmer? I don't know that name."

"That's the baby elephant's name. I heard it from some of the other students," Marcus explained. "It's really unfortunate, he's such a young and innocent animal."

Ethan felt a pang of worry in his chest. "Do they know what caused it?"

Marcus shook his head. "Not yet, but I heard they're doing everything they can to figure out what happened and save him."

The two friends sat in silence for a moment, both lost in their own thoughts about the poor elephant and the unknown dangers that could threaten the animal inhabitants of the Sanctuary.

CHAPTER 8

LESSONS IN STRATEGY

The morning sun was just beginning to peek over the horizon as Ethan made his way to the main building of the Sanctuary. The crisp air nipped at his nose, and he could see his breath in front of him as he walked. As he rounded the corner, he saw Emma sitting on a bench outside the building, her backpack at her feet and a huge grin on her face.

Emma was practically bouncing with excitement. "I can't wait for Mr. Black's class! I heard he's the best at teaching us how to use our abilities in combat."

Ethan, on the other hand, wasn't as thrilled. "I don't know, Em. I'm not really into the whole fighting thing. Plus, Marcus said he didn't want to take this class, so I don't know if it's really for me."

Emma rolled her eyes playfully. "Come on, Ethan. Mr. Black is like, super cool. And he's a gorilla Animalian. How awesome is that?"

Ethan shrugged. "I guess it's worth a shot. In fact, I'm only doing this class because I saw Mr. Black's name on it. Plus, I heard he's pretty ripped, so maybe I'll learn some muscles tips."

Emma punched Ethan lightly on the arm. "You're such a dork, but I'm glad you're coming. It's going to be so much fun!"

Mr. Black's classroom was located in the main training building of the Sanctuary. The room was spacious, with high ceilings and large windows that let in natural light. The walls were painted a deep gray color, and there were several posters of different animal powers and techniques displayed on them. The floor was made of hardwood and was polished to a shine. There was a large open space in the middle of the room, where students practice their techniques, and the walls were lined with mirrors, which allowed students to see their movements and correct any mistakes. There were also several mats placed around the room, where students could take a break or sit and watch their classmates during training. Overall, the classroom had a functional and serious atmosphere, reflecting the nature of the class and the instructor.

"Welcome back, Ethan," Mr. Black said, a smile spreading across his face. "It's been a while since we last saw each other. How have you been enjoying your time at the Sanctuary?"

Ethan smiled back, feeling a certain familiarity with the gorilla Animalian. "It's been great, Mr. Black. I've learned a lot and made some new friends. I'm excited to be in your class."

"I'm glad to hear that," Mr. Black said, his voice rumbling. "I remember when I first recruited you to the Sanctuary a few months ago, you were just a shy kid with a lot of potential. It's great to see how much you've grown since then already."

Ethan blushed at the compliment, feeling a sense of pride.

Mr. Black turned to Emma, his gaze lingering on her for a moment. "And Emma, I've heard you're quite the strong one. I can't wait to see what you're capable of."

Emma smiled, her face flushing. She was excited to be in this class and to learn from someone as experienced as Mr. Black.

"Let's get started!" Mr. Black exclaimed, clapping his hands together.

Mr. Black stood at the front of the classroom, his broad shoulders and imposing presence commanding attention. "Welcome, students," he boomed, his deep voice filling the room. "This is Combat Training. It's important to remember that we are not here to learn how to hurt others, but to defend ourselves and those we love. Our powers are a gift, but they can also be a danger if misused. I expect all of you to follow safety protocols and to never use your powers against humans unless it is a matter of life and death."

Ethan listened intently, feeling excitement and anxiety building inside him. Although hesitant at first, he had heard great things about Mr. Black and was eager to learn from such a skilled and powerful warrior.

Mr. Black began his class by discussing the importance of proper control over one's powers. He emphasized that while it may be tempting to use their abilities recklessly, it is crucial to always consider the safety of oneself and others. He then delved into the topic of defense, explaining the various ways in which Animalians could use their powers to protect themselves and their loved ones. He also touched on the subject of the use of powers against humans, stressing the importance of only using them in self-defense and in situations where it was absolutely necessary. Mr. Black's words were clear and concise, and he effectively conveyed the importance of these topics to his students.

"Alright students, now that we've covered some of the basics, it's time to put them into practice. I want you all to find a partner to work with. The goal here is to grapple your opponent to the ground. Look for someone with a similar level of strength as yourself. Remember, safety is our top priority. We're here to learn how to defend ourselves, not hurt each other," Mr. Black said, his voice echoed throughout the room. Emma jokingly raised her hand and said, "Hey Mr. Black, can I be Ethan's partner? I promise I won't hurt him too much." Ethan playfully rolled his eyes and responded, "Yeah right, I don't want to be your practice dummy, Em." The class chuckled at the playful banter between the two friends.

Ethan scanned the room, looking for a suitable partner to practice with. His eyes fell on a small, skinny boy sitting in the corner. He didn't know the boy's name, but he figured he would be a good match since they seemed to have a similar build. "Hey, I'm Ethan, can I partner up with you?" Ethan asked, approaching the boy.

The boy looked up, surprised. "I'm Alex, but I don't know, maybe I should find someone else...," Alex replied with hesitation.

"Don't worry, I won't hurt you," Ethan said, wearing a confident smirk.

Mr. Black, who had been observing the room, stepped in. "Are you sure about that, Ethan? I don't want anyone to get hurt," he said, concern etched on his face.

Ethan interrupted him with a wave of his hand. "I got this, Mr. Black. Alex and I will be fine," he said, giving Alex a confident smile.

Alex smiled back, "Okay, we got this. Don't worry Mr. Black."

Ethan and Alex stood across from each other, both looking focused and determined. They start to circle each other, looking for an opening. Suddenly, Alex lunges forward, his small frame moving very fast. He grabs hold of Ethan's arm and twists it behind his back, lifting him off the ground with one hand. Ethan's eyes widen in surprise as he is thrown to the ground with a thud.

"What was that?" Ethan asks, confusion etched on his face.

Alex grins, "I've got ant-like strength, I can carry 20 times my body weight!"

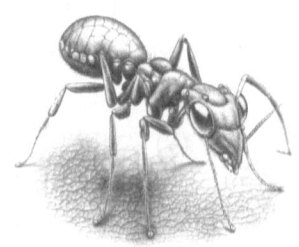

Ethan nods, impressed despite the embarrassment of being thrown so easily. Mr. Black watches the exchange, a small smile on his face as he sees Ethan's determination to improve.

"Nice work, Alex. Keep it up," he says, turning his attention to the rest of the class.

As Ethan and Alex continued to grapple, Alex easily picked Ethan up and threw him to the ground again. Ethan was starting to feel frustrated and confused. He couldn't understand how he could win over such strong adversary. He started to question the purpose of the class and if he was even cut out for it.

"How are you doing this?" Ethan asked, panting and sweating.

"It's all about leverage," Alex replied with a grin. "I may not be as big as you, but I know how to use my strength effectively."

Ethan nodded, trying to absorb this new information. He felt a twinge of embarrassment as Alex took him down again, but he knew that he needed to learn from this experience.

Thud!

As Ethan lay on the mat, feeling defeated yet again, Mr. Black approached him with a stern look on his face. "Ethan, you need to make use of your strengths," he said firmly. "I've heard that you're fast, so why aren't you using that to your advantage?"

Ethan sat up, feeling a bit frustrated. "But I'm not strong," he protested.

Mr. Black shook his head. "I'm not talking about brute force, Ethan. I'm talking about using what you have to your advantage. Leverage your speed, use it to outmaneuver your opponents. You have to learn to adapt, to think on your feet."

Ethan nodded, understanding the lesson. "I'll try," he said, determined to do better.

"That's all I ask," Mr. Black replied, giving him a pat on the back. "Now, let's get back to training."

Ethan and Alex squared off again, and this time, Ethan was determined to put Mr. Black's advice into practice. He began by darting around the perimeter of the ring, using his speed to stay just out of Alex's reach. Alex, with his ant-like strength, lunged forward again and again, but each time, Ethan was able to evade him.

As the match progressed, Ethan started to get a feel for Alex's movements and patterns. He noticed that Alex had a tendency to overcommit on his grabs, leaving himself open for a counterattack. Taking advantage of this, Ethan began to use his speed to slip in and out of Alex's grasp, poking him with quick jabs and kicks.

Alex was getting frustrated, and his movements became more and more wild. Ethan, however, remained calm and focused. He continued to use his speed to his advantage, darting around the ring and striking Alex whenever he had the opportunity.

Finally, as Alex lunged forward for yet another grab, Ethan saw his chance. He sidestepped Alex's grasp and, in one fluid motion, swept his leg out from under him. Alex hit the ground hard with a thud, and Ethan stood victorious.

Mr. Black approached Ethan, a look of pride on his face. "Well done, Ethan," he said, clapping him on the shoulder. "You've learned to leverage your strengths and use them to your advantage. That's what being a true warrior is all about."

Ethan grinned, feeling a sense of accomplishment. He had come into the class thinking that he was weak and insignificant, but now he realized that he had something valuable to offer. He had speed, and he was going to use it to the best of his abilities.

After the intense grapple, Ethan helped Alex up. "Are you okay?" Ethan asked with concern, noticing that Alex was rubbing his back.

"Yeah, I'm fine," Alex said with a chuckle, "I'm just not used to being the one on the ground."

Ethan couldn't help but laugh, "Yeah, been there."

"Don't worry about it," Alex said with a grin, "You were pretty impressive out there. I've never seen anyone move like that before."

"Thanks," Ethan said, feeling prideful.

"You know, I've always been strong, but I never really knew how to use it," Alex said, "I guess we both have something to learn from each other."

Ethan nodded in agreement, "Yeah, I think we do."

The two boys stood there for a moment, smiling at each other. Despite their intense grapple, there was a mood of camaraderie between them. They had just met, but they already felt like they were becoming friends.

As Emma and Ethan walked out of the combat class, they were greeted by the familiar faces of the Stone brothers, Jake, Tyler, and Zack. The triplets were leaning against the wall, looking cool and collected as usual. But as soon as they saw Emma and Ethan, their expressions changed. They smirked and started to mock them.

"Hey look, it's the weaklings," Jake sneered.

Ethan shook his head and tried to ignore them, but Emma was not one to back down. She stood up tall and glared at the brothers.

"What do you want, Stone brothers?" Emma said, her voice cold and menacing.

The brothers laughed, their bravado faltering slightly as they remembered the last time they had crossed Emma.

"Just making conversation," Tyler said, trying to sound nonchalant.

"Well, we don't have time for your crap," Emma said, pushing past them.

But the brothers weren't done yet. They continued to provoke and mock Emma and Ethan, until Emma had enough. She grabbed Jake by the collar and lifted him off the ground.

"You want to mess with us? Fine, but you better watch your back," Emma growled.

Just then, a staff member noticed the commotion and intervened. They separated Emma and Jake, and sent Emma and Ethan to detention for their actions.

As they walked to detention, Ethan noticed the satisfied grins on the faces of the Stone brothers. It dawned on him that their provocation must have been part of their plan all along. Emma, on the other hand, was trying to explain her actions to the staff member, a tall, middle-aged woman with short, curly hair and kind eyes. She had a stern expression on her face, but Ethan could tell she was trying to understand Emma's perspective. The woman's name was Ms. Jenkins and she was known for her fairness and strict adherence to the rules. Despite Emma's attempts to justify herself, Ms. Jenkins firmly insisted that they serve detention as a warning to not let their emotions get the best of them in the future.

CHAPTER 9

CANINE CONSEQUENCES

Ethan and Emma's detention was in an open area, surrounded by tall wooden fences. The sun was shining bright and the birds were chirping, making it a beautiful day. Ethan and Emma walked in, accompanied by Doug, who was their supervisor for the detention. Doug greeted them with a big smile and a wave, "Welcome to detention, guys. Today we'll be helping out with the feeding and cleaning of the dogs and other canids. It's a beautiful day and the animals will be happy to have some company."

Ethan and Emma looked around and saw that there were no cages. Instead, they saw large open fields filled with different types of dogs, foxes and even wolves and coyotes roaming freely. Some were playing, while others were lying in the sun. There were also several large kennels and shelters scattered around the area.

"Wow, this is amazing," Emma said, impressed by the sight.

"Yeah, it's a great place to spend detention," Doug said with a chuckle. "Don't worry, it's not as bad as it sounds. You'll be helping out with the care of these beautiful animals and it's a great opportunity to learn about them."

Ethan and Emma nodded, eager to start. Doug led them to a nearby shelter where they began to help with the feeding and cleaning of the animals. As they worked, Doug chatted with them about the different types of animals they were caring for and shared some interesting facts and stories about them.

"Hey, what brings you two here? I've never imagine I'd see you two in detention, at least not so soon," Doug asked, a friendly smile on his face.

"It's a long story," Emma grumbled, still clearly upset about the whole situation.

Ethan chimed in, "Basically, the Stone brothers set us up and we got caught up in their prank."

"Those little punks," Doug said, shaking his head. "I've had run-ins with them before. They're always causing trouble. But don't worry, detention isn't so bad. It's actually kind of nice to have a break from classes and get to spend some time with the animals."

Emma rolled her eyes, "I guess it's not so bad, but I still can't believe we fell for their trick."

Ethan nodded in agreement. "Yeah, it's a bummer but at least we're not in trouble with the staff. And it's pretty cool getting to take care of all these dogs and other animals."

Doug grinned, "Exactly! And hey, you also get to spend some time with me," he added with a laugh.

The three of them continued their work, chatting and joking as they went about their tasks. Despite the unfortunate circumstances that brought them there, they found themselves enjoying the company and the opportunity to bond with the animals.

Ethan couldn't help but notice the way Doug seemed to take in every scent and sound around him. "Man, it must be nice to have these super sense and stuff, right?"

Doug grinned and nodded. "Yeah, it's these dog-like senses, I've got a pretty good sense of smell and hearing. It comes in handy for tracking, and stuff like that."

Emma chimed in, "I've seen him track scents that were days old. It's pretty impressive."

Doug chuckled, "Yeah, it's definitely a unique talent. But I'm not the only one with a special ability here. What about you two?"

Ethan and Emma exchanged a glance before Ethan spoke up. "I'm a falcon Animalian," he said, shrugging. "I can run pretty fast and jump really high. I'm still figuring it all out, though."

Emma grinned. "I'm a bear Animalian," she said, flexing her arms playfully. "I've got some serious strength."

"Oh, so you're like a bird and a bear? Cool! I've never met a falcon Animalian before, that's pretty awesome. And you, Emma, a bear? Girl, you must be one strong lady," Doug said with a playful grin.

"Yeah, I'm still learning how to use it," Ethan said, shrugging. "But it's cool to have something unique."

"Definitely," Emma agreed. "I've had my bear powers for a while now, so I'm pretty used to them. It's just part of who I am."

Doug nodded, impressed. "Well, it's cool to have you both here. I'm sure you'll both be kicking butt in no time."

Ethan and Emma laughed, feeling at ease with Doug's casual and friendly attitude. They all continued to chat and clean up the area, enjoying each other's company.

As the detention time was coming to an end, Doug turned to Ethan and Emma and said, "Alright guys, we're almost done here. I just need you to grab that bag of food over there and bring it to the coyote pen." He pointed to a large bag of food sitting on a nearby shelf.

Ethan and Emma quickly grabbed the bag and followed Doug to the coyote pen. The pen was a large open area filled with various types of coyotes. Some were lounging in the sun while others were running around, playing with each other.

"Okay, just throw the food in there and they'll take care of the rest," Doug said with a grin.

Ethan and Emma tossed the bag of food into the pen and watched as the coyotes descended upon it, eagerly devouring the food.

"Wow, they sure are hungry," Emma commented.

"Yeah, they're always hungry. But don't worry, they'll be well fed now," Doug said with a chuckle. "Thanks for your help, guys. I'll see you next time."

As Ethan and Emma were leaving the detention, they discussed their plans for the rest of the day. Suddenly, they heard Doug's voice crying for help. They immediately rushed back to the area where they had been working, their hearts pounding with fear and concern. When they arrived, they found Doug standing in the middle of the pen, surrounded by the coyotes they had just fed. All of the animals were lying motionless on the ground, clearly unconscious.

Doug's face was pale with shock and fear. "I don't know what happened," he stammered, his voice trembling. "we gave them the food like I always do, and then they just... collapsed."

Ethan and Emma quickly scanned the area, looking for any signs of what could have caused this. But there was nothing out of the ordinary to be seen.

"We need to get help," Emma said urgently.

Ethan and Emma approached the headmaster's office with a sense of trepidation. The office was located in the main administrative building of the Sanctuary, and it was a large, imposing structure made of stone and marble. As they walked up the steps to the entrance, Ethan felt the anxiety in the pit of his stomach. He had never been called to the headmaster's office before, and he wasn't sure what to expect.

As they entered the building, they were greeted by a grand foyer with a high ceiling and marble flooring. The walls were adorned with paintings and tapestries, and there were several statues and sculptures on display. But one statue in particular caught his attention. It was a statue of a warrior with a big spear in hand, and next to him was a fierce lion. The details of the statue were exquisite, from the intricate patterns on the warrior's clothes to the individual hairs on the lion's mane. The air was filled with the sound of soft classical music, and the lighting was dim, giving the space a vibe of elegance and sophistication.

Ethan and Emma walked up to the reception desk, where a woman in a smart business suit greeted them with a smile. She asked them to take a seat and wait while she let the headmaster know they had arrived. Ethan and Emma sat down on the plush velvet chairs, and Ethan felt out of place. He had never been in such a grand and opulent space before, and he felt small and insignificant in comparison.

As they waited, Ethan's mind wondered what caused the headmaster to summon them. Had they done something wrong? Was he in trouble? He couldn't shake the feeling of unease and uncertainty that hung over him like a cloud.

Finally, the receptionist informed them that the headmaster was ready to see them, and they were led to his office. Ethan's thoughts were racing as they reached the door. He couldn't help but think that they were being accused of something, and that this was going to be the end of their time at the Sanctuary. First the detention and now this. Emma seemed to sense his thoughts, and she gave him a reassuring pat on the shoulder.

The office was even more grand and imposing than the foyer, with a large mahogany desk in the center of the room and floor-to-ceiling windows that looked out over the Sanctuary grounds. The headmaster, Leo Braveheart, stood up from his desk to greet them. He was an imposing figure, tall and well-built, with a distinguished and regal look. Ethan felt a sense of respect in his presence.

Braveheart welcomed them and asked if they knew why they were there.

Ethan and Emma exchanged confused glances, and then Emma spoke up, "No, sir. We don't know why we're here."

Braveheart's expression softened, "I understand that this must be confusing for you. You see, there have been some recent incidents involving the poisoning of some of our animals. You were both present during both of these incidents, and I was hoping..."

Emma's expression turned to one of alarm, "Are you suspecting us, sir? We had nothing to do with what happened to the animals!" She said, interrupting the headmaster.

Braveheart held up his hand, "Please, Emma. I'm not suspecting you of anything. I just need to gather as much information as possible. Any hint or clue that you can provide, no matter how small, could be of great help to us. Did you see anything unusual? Anyone acting in a strange manner?"

Ethan felt his heart race as Braveheart spoke. He knew that he and Emma were innocent, but he still had a sensation of guilt. He knew that they were at the wrong place at the wrong time, but he couldn't shake the feeling that they were being blamed for something they didn't do.

Ethan spoke up, "Sir, we didn't see anything. We were just in the wrong place at the wrong time."

Braveheart gave a small nod, "I understand. But if you think of anything, anything at all, please come to me immediately."

Ethan and Emma nodded, both relieved that they were not being blamed but still worried about what was happening in the Sanctuary.

"Excuse me, Mr. Braveheart," Emma spoke up, her voice shaking slightly, "but do you know what's causing the poisonings? Is there a cure?"

"We're not sure yet what is causing the poisonings," Braveheart said, his voice serious and grave. "But we suspect that someone is deliberately contaminating the animals' food. The poison that we found in the animals' blood is a variation of a very potent and rare venom, and we don't know what the long-term effects will be. To find a cure, we need to find out who or what is causing it."

Ethan's mind raced as he tried to process the information. He had never heard of anything like this happening before at the Sanctuary. "Do you have any leads or suspects?" he asked, his voice trembling slightly.

Braveheart shook his head. "Not yet, but we're investigating all possibilities. We're doing everything we can to keep our residents safe and to find the source of the contamination."

Emma leaned forward, her eyes determined. "What can we do to help?" she asked.

"Right now, the best thing you can do is to be vigilant," Braveheart replied. "Report any suspicious activity or unusual behavior to me immediately. And, above all, be careful what you eat or drink. We don't know how the poison is being delivered, so we have to be cautious."

Ethan and Emma nodded, both feeling responsible to do their part in helping to solve the mystery. They left Braveheart's office, their minds filled with thoughts of the poisonings and the unknown dangers that lurked within the Sanctuary.

CHAPTER 10

THE ELEPHANT AND THE SNAKE

Marcus and Ethan's dorm room was small but cozy, with a twin bed pushed against the wall and a small desk with a lamp on each side of the room. Ethan's walls were adorned with multiple photographies he took throughout the years and a framed picture of Ethan and his family. Emma and Marcus were sitting on the bed, listening intently as Ethan recounted the events of the day.

"So, Mr. Black is like, 'Use your strengths, Ethan.' And I'm like, 'But I'm not strong.' And he's like, 'I'm not talking about brute force. I heard you're fast.' And I was like, 'Oh.' And then

I sweep kicked Alex to the ground. It was awesome." Ethan said, a hint of excitement in his voice.

"That's so cool, Ethan," Emma said, her eyes sparkling with admiration. "I wish I could move like that."

"Yeah, but then we got sent to detention," Ethan said, his excitement fading.

"Wow, that's crazy," Marcus said, leaning back in his chair. "But why were you guys sent to detention? I don't get it."

"The Stone brothers," Emma said, her tone bitter. "It was all a set up. They were provoking us and acting all innocent, and when I finally defended myself, they made it look like we were the aggressors."

Marcus shook his head in disbelief. "The Stone brothers, huh? They're notorious for pulling stunts like that. It's like the old saying goes, 'the best defense is a good offense'."

Ethan looked confused. "What does that mean?"

"It means," Marcus explained, "that the Stone brothers knew that Emma was stronger than them, so they figured if they could provoke her into attacking them, they'd be able to turn the tables and make it look like they were the victims. Classic 'play the victim' strategy."

"I had no idea," Ethan said, feeling a little foolish.

"Don't feel bad, man," Marcus said, clapping him on the shoulder. "It's not something that's taught in school. But now you know, and you can be prepared for it next time."

Emma nodded in agreement.

"So we were put in charge of feeding and cleaning up after the canines," Emma began, "and it was actually kind of fun. We got to play with some of the dogs and even got to help with training a few of them."

Ethan chimed in, "Yeah, and Doug was there too. He's a funny guy."

Marcus nodded in understanding, "That's pretty cool I guess."

"Yeah, it was pretty cool," Emma continued, "But then something strange happened. We were finishing up and getting ready to leave when Doug suddenly cried for help. We rushed back and found all the coyotes we had just fed laying unconscious on the ground."

Ethan added, "It was crazy. We had no idea what was happening and neither did Doug. We were so confused and worried. We didn't know if they were going to be okay."

Marcus's expression turned serious, "That sounds really strange. I wonder if it has something to do with Elmer's poisoning."

Ethan and Emma nodded, "We were thinking the same thing. We went to talk to Braveheart about it but he didn't really have any answers for us. He just said they were trying to figure out what was going on and that they needed to find the source of the poison."

"That's really concerning," Marcus said, "We need to figure out what's going on soon before anyone else gets hurt. This is like a real-life mystery," he exclaimed, his eyes lighting up with excitement. "Did you guys see anything unusual while you were helping out with the animals? Any clues or hints about who might be behind it?" he asked eagerly, turning to Ethan and Emma.

Emma sat back on the bed and shook her head, "We didn't see anything unusual. We already told that to Braveheart." She let out a sigh, "I'm still so confused about everything. I didn't even know that animals could be poisoned like that."

Marcus leaned forward in his chair, a look of determination on his face. "Well, we've got to figure out what's going on. We can't just sit around and do nothing. We need to find some clues, gather some evidence."

Ethan nodded in agreement.

Suddenly, Ethan remembered a detail he had forgotten. "Wait, I think I remember something." he said. "At Animal Communication class I saw a boy rushing out as soon as the bell rang. He was limping, like he was injured."

Marcus's eyes lit up. "Do you remember who it was?" he asked eagerly.

Ethan shook his head. "No, I'm sorry. I didn't get a good look at his face."

"Well, that's something to go on," Marcus said. "If only we could go back in time to see who he was."

"Yeah, that would be great," Emma said.

"Hey, I have an idea," Marcus said. "What about talking to Michael?"

"Who's Michael?" Ethan asked, looking confused.

"He's the elephant Animalian boy who was communicating with Elmer. He might have more information," Marcus explained.

"You know, I think that's a good idea," Emma spoke, her expression showing signs of fatigue from the day's events. "We should talk to Michael first thing in the morning and see if he knows anything that can help us figure out what's going on."

Emma announced that it was getting late and she should head back to her dorm.

"Goodnight, guys," she said, giving them each a quick hug. "Let's solve this mystery tomorrow."

"Good night, Em," replied Ethan. With that, she slipped out of the room and closed the door behind her.

Ethan reached over to the light switch, his hand hovering over it as he turned to Marcus. "Do you want me to leave the light on for you?" he asked. Marcus shook his head and grinned. "I can read in the dark," he said with a chuckle. Ethan nodded and flipped the switch, plunging the room into darkness. "What a great roommate to have," he thought.

The three friends met early in the morning in the bustling cafeteria. The room was filled with students of all ages, chatting and laughing as they ate their breakfast. Emma scanned the crowd, looking for Michael. "How are we going to find him in this sea of people?" she asked.

Marcus shrugged. "Don't worry, Ethan's got this," he said, nodding towards his friend.

Ethan grinned. "Yeah, no problem," he said. "I'm a falcon Animalian, I can spot every single person in this room with ease."

With that, Ethan scanned the crowd, his sharp eyes scanning the room. After a moment, he pointed. "There he is," he said, pointing to a short, chubby boy with short hair. "That's Michael."

The three friends made their way over to where Michael was sitting. As they approached, Michael looked up and smiled. "Hey, guys," he said. "What's up?"

"We were hoping to talk to you about something," Emma said. "Do you have a minute?"

"Sure," Michael said, gesturing for them to sit. "What's on your mind?"

Ethan explained that they were trying to find out who was behind the recent poisonings at the Sanctuary and they wanted to know if Michael had seen anything unusual in the day of Elmer's poisoning or if he had any information that could help.

"I'm sorry, guys," Michael said, his voice heavy with emotion. "I wish I could tell you more, but I haven't seen anything out of the ordinary."

"That's okay, Michael. We were just wondering if you remember who got close to Elmer that day," Ethan asked.

"Of course I remember, I always remember everything," Michael replied, his eyes distant as he thought back. "It was a boy named Jack. He was petting Elmer and he insisted on helping feeding him."

Ethan leaned in, his interest piqued. "Do you remember if Jack was limping that day?"

Michael nodded. "Yeah, now that you mention it, I do remember him limping. I thought it was strange at the time, but I didn't think much of it."

"That's it!" Emma exclaimed, her eyes lighting up with recognition. "I know who Jack is! He's a snake Animalian, I bet Elmer must have bitten or harmed him in some way and he took revenge, like snakes do."

Ethan and Marcus looked at each other in surprise. "Are you sure?" Marcus asked.

"Positive," Emma replied confidently. "I've had a few classes with him and I know he can be vengeful."

"But why would he poison all the other animals?" Ethan asked.

"I don't know, that's a good question," Emma said, "But we need to find out. Let's go talk to him."

The three of them quickly stood up from their seats and rushed out of the cafeteria without a word to Michael. They were too focused on their new lead and the urgency to confront Jack and get to the bottom of the poisonings. Michael sat alone at the table, watching as they disappeared into the crowd of students, feeling a bit confused and hurt by their sudden departure. They made their way to the classroom where Jack's first class of the day was. As they walked, Ethan felt a sense of unease. If Emma was right, and Jack was responsible for the poisonings, then they were dealing with a dangerous individual. But he knew that they had to get to the bottom of this, for the sake of all the animals at the Sanctuary.

Ethan, Marcus and Emma entered the classroom, their eyes scanning the room for Jack. They saw him sitting at his desk, scribbling in a notebook. He had dark, greasy hair that was slicked back, and his face had a sly grin on it. He was wearing a leather jacket and jeans, and he had a sneer on his face as he looked up at the trio.

"Jack, we need to talk to you," Emma said, her voice firm.

"What about?" Jack sneered, looking up at them.

"About Elmer," Ethan said, his voice low. "We know you did something to him."

"I don't know what you're talking about," Jack said, his grin widening. "I never even been to that class. I only heard about what happened to Elmer."

"Don't lie to us, Jack," Marcus said, his voice cold. "We know you're a snake Animalian, and we know you have a grudge against Elmer."

"I have no grudge against Elmer," Jack said, his grin faltering. "I never even met the guy."

"Don't play dumb, Jack," Emma said, her voice filled with anger. "We know you're behind this, and we won't rest until we find out the truth."

"I have nothing to do with this," Jack said, his grin disappearing completely. "I swear, I don't know anything about Elmer or his poisoning."

Suddenly, they heard a loud voice from the back of the room. "Watch out! Emma is bullying another kid again!" They turned to see the Stone brothers, Jake, Tyler and Zack, standing up from their seats, grins on their faces. The rest of the class turned to look at Emma, confusion and disapproval on their faces. Emma's face turned red with embarrassment and anger.

"That's not true!" Emma exclaimed, trying to defend herself. "We were just trying to talk to Jack about something that happened in the Sanctuary."

"Yeah, sure," Jake sneered. "Just like how you 'talked' to us yesterday."

The rest of the class began to murmur and side-eye Emma, making her feel even more upset and small.

"This is not fair!" Emma said, her voice shaking with emotion. "You know what really happened yesterday and you're just trying to make me look bad."

But no one was listening to her, they believed in the Stone brothers words and Emma couldn't do anything but feel very sad and upset.

Just then, Mr. Black entered the room and asked, "What is going on here?" The room fell silent as the students turned to face their teacher. Mr. Black's gaze settled on Emma, Ethan and Marcus, and he beckoned for them to come forward. "I would like to speak with you three in private," he said.

The trio followed Mr. Black out of the classroom and into a small office. As soon as the door closed, Mr. Black turned to them and said, "What is this I am hearing about Emma bullying another student? First you two go to detention and now this?"

Mr. Black listened attentively as Ethan and Marcus explained their findings about Elmer and Jack. Emma sat quietly, tears welling up in her eyes as she felt ashamed of being labeled as a bully.

"So let me get this straight," Mr. Black said, his brow furrowed in concentration. "You believe that Jack, who is a snake Animalian, was responsible for poisoning Elmer, the baby elephant?"

Ethan nodded. "That's what we think. We talked to Michael, the elephant Animalian who was communicating with Elmer, and he said that Jack was petting Elmer and insisted on helping to feed him. And we also know that Jack is a snake Animalian, and snakes are known for their venom. Also, I saw Jack rushing out the class as soon as it ended. But he is denying everything," he explained.

Mr. Black shook his head. "I'm sorry, but I just can't believe that Jack would be capable of something like this," he said, his voice stern but also tinged with disappointment. "You three should know better than to go around accusing other people without solid evidence. If you know something, you should come to me or Headmaster Braveheart right away. We can't have students accusing each other without proper cause." The trio looked down, feeling guilty for jumping to conclusions about Jack.

He turned to Emma, his expression softening. "And Emma, I know you're not a bully. But even good people can make mistakes and do things they regret. I know this from personal experience."

Mr. Black let out a sigh, his eyes distant as he remembered his own past. "When I was a student here at the Sanctuary, I liked this girl. But another boy, Leon, also had feelings for her. I did things that I deeply regret now, and it wasn't until years later that I learned the terrible things that happened to him. I feel guilty to this day, and I wish I could apologize for what I did, but he's no longer with us."

He looked back at Emma, Ethan and Marcus, his gaze firm. "My point is, don't make the same mistakes I did. If you know something, come talk to me or Braveheart. And make amends with Jack and the Stone brothers."

CHAPTER 11

FOLLOWING THE SCENT

The following days, Emma, Marcus, and Ethan decided to keep an eye on Jack, determined to find out if he was really responsible for Elmer's poisoning. They followed him around the Sanctuary, watching his every move and trying to catch him in the act.

"So, what's the plan?" Emma asked as they staked out around a corner.

"We just have to keep an eye on him and see if he does anything suspicious," Ethan replied, scanning the crowd for any sign of Jack's malice.

"Yeah, and maybe we'll get lucky and he'll slip up and reveal himself as the snake he is," Marcus added with a chuckle.

But as the time went on, it became clear that Jack wasn't showing any signs of guilt. He went about his business as usual, attending classes and hanging out with his friends. He didn't seem to be limping either.

"I don't know, guys. Maybe we're wrong about him," Emma said, looking dejected.

"What should we do now?" Emma asked, looking frustrated. "Dress up like animals and ambush the criminal?"

"Ha ha, very funny," Marcus replied with a chuckle. "But seriously, we don't have any other leads."

Ethan sighed. "I know. I was really sure it was Jack. But maybe we're just grasping at straws."

"Hey, I have an idea," Emma said, sitting up straight. "Why don't we go talk to Doug? He's the one with the dog-like senses, maybe he can help us find more information."

"That's a great idea," Marcus said, nodding. "And we can also check on him and see how he's doing."

Ethan nodded. "Yeah, let's do that. I haven't seen him since detention. I hope he's okay."

The three of them stood up and headed towards the animal sanctuary, where they knew they would find Doug. They were determined to get to the bottom of this mystery, even if it meant talking to every person and animal in the Sanctuary.

As Emma, Ethan, and Marcus walked towards the animal care area of the Sanctuary, they could hear the soft barking and whining of the canines. As they got closer, they saw Doug sitting on the ground, surrounded by a pack of dogs. He looked up as they approached and gave them a small smile, but they could tell he was upset.

"Hey guys," Doug said, "I'm just hanging out with my buddies here. Trying to take my mind off what happened with the coyotes."

The trio sat down next to him, with Emma patting a friendly-looking golden retriever on the head. "We're so sorry about what happened, Doug," Ethan said.

"Yeah, it's really terrible," Marcus added. "We just wanted to check on you and see if there was anything we could do to help."

Doug shook his head. "I appreciate it, but there's not much anyone can do. The coyotes were poisoned, they are still unconscious, and we still don't know how or why."

Ethan leaned forward, his eyes serious. "Actually, that's kind of why we wanted to talk to you. We've been trying to figure out who might be behind the poisonings, and we were wondering if you noticed anything strange or out of the ordinary."

Doug thought for a moment, scratching the ears of a nearby German Shepherd. "I wish I had more information for you guys," he said. "But I haven't seen or heard anything suspicious. I've just been focusing on taking care of the animals here."

Ethan then stepped forward. "Doug, what about on the day of the poisoning. Did you hear or smell anything unusual?"

Doug paused for a moment, thinking. "Now that you mention it, I do remember smelling a unique scent that day. It's something I've only smelled once before. It was a bit sweet, but also had a hint of something spicy. I can't quite put my finger on it," Doug replied, furrowing his brow in concentration.

"Hmm, that's strange. Do you remember where you smelled it before?" Ethan asked.

"Yeah, it was during this year's welcoming speech by Braveheart. Sarah from the 10th grade was standing near me and I smelled it on her," Doug said.

Marcus's face lit up. "Sarah? You mean Sarah Williams? The one with the blonde hair and green eyes?"

"Yeah, that's her," Doug confirmed.

"Wow, that's really interesting," Emma said, exchanging a glance with Ethan and Marcus. "But it probably doesn't mean anything, right?"

Doug shook his head. "I don't know, but I don't think so. Sarah seems like a nice girl, I can't imagine her being involved in something like this."

"Thanks for the information, Doug," Marcus said, trying to hide his excitement. "We'll look into it and let you know if we find anything."

"Sure thing," Doug said, returning his attention to the canines. "I just hope we can figure out what's going on and catch the person responsible."

Ethan, Emma and Marcus left the kennel, their minds racing with the new information they had just received. Marcus couldn't help but think about Sarah and how he had always had a crush on her, but he knew they had to focus on the task at hand.

The trio sat in a quiet corner of the cafeteria, discussing their next move in their investigation. Marcus was particularly excited about the prospect of talking to Sarah Williams, a girl who had caught his eye.

"I think we should talk to Sarah," Marcus said, his voice filled with determination. "I know she's not the culprit, but she might have some information that could help us. I want to lead the conversation this time and make sure we don't accuse anyone without solid evidence."

Ethan and Emma exchanged a knowing glance, both noticing Marcus' abrupt enthusiasm in Sarah. "Why the sudden interest in Sarah?" Emma asked with a smirk.

Marcus blushed a little and shrugged. "It's nothing, really. I just think she might be able to help us somehow."

Ethan nodded, understanding where Marcus was coming from. "Alright, we'll talk to Sarah. But we need to be careful and make sure we don't jump to any conclusions."

"Agreed," Emma chimed in. "Let's make a plan and approach this conversation in a calm and collected manner."

Marcus quickly stood up, "H-hi Sarah, how are you?" He stuttered.

Coincidentally, Sarah was walking by the table where Emma, Marcus and Ethan were sitting. She was a petite girl with long blonde hair and green eyes, she was wearing a pair of glasses that made her look even more intelligent.

She looked at Marcus with surprise, she had never talked to him before. "Hi, I'm good, thanks. And you?" She replied politely.

"I'm fine, thanks," Marcus said, still feeling nervous. He then introduced her to Emma and Ethan, "This is Emma and Ethan, we're in the same grade."

"Nice to meet you," Sarah said with a smile.

The trio and Sarah had an awkward silence for a moment, until Marcus finally gathered the courage to start a conversation. "So, we were just talking about the recent poisonings that have been happening in the Sanctuary," he said, trying to sound casual.

Sarah's expression changed, becoming more serious. "Yes, I've heard about that. I've been doing some research on it, and the symptoms of the poisoning seem to be similar to the venom found in some reptiles."

Emma interjected, "Really? That's interesting. What do you know about it?"

Sarah replied, "Well, the venom causes paralysis and incapacitates the victim. It's very potent and fast-acting, and it's usually found in snakes and lizards."

Ethan chipped in, "Do you think it's possible that someone is using this venom to poison the animals in the Sanctuary?"

Sarah nodded, "It's definitely a possibility. But there are also other types of toxins and poisons that can cause similar symptoms. It's hard to say for sure without more information. Do you know anything about that?"

Marcus began to explain what they knew, but Emma cut him off, her voice cold and suspicious. "We're not sure what to believe yet," Emma said. "We're still trying to figure out what's going on."

Sarah nodded, understanding the skepticism in Emma's tone. Ethan then asked her if she saw or smelled anything unusual during Braveheart's welcoming speech. Sarah shook her head, "I actually arrived late and missed the speech. I'm sorry I can't be of much help."

The trio looked at each other, perplexed.

"Well, Sarah, we're not sure about much, but we do know that you're the smartest girl in school. Maybe you can help us figure this whole thing out?" Marcus said, with an exaggerated grin.

Sarah blushes a little and says "I'll do my best to help once you trust me with all the information you have. Oh, and by the way, I didn't catch your name."

"M-Marcus!" Marcus stuttered, realizing he had never actually introduced himself.

Marcus, who had been so eager to talk to her, suddenly found himself at a loss for words. Emma, who had been suspicious of Sarah from the start, simply nodded in response. Ethan, who had been the one to ask about Braveheart's speech, also didn't know what to say.

"Well, I'll see you later then," Sarah said, noticing the discomfort.

"Yeah, see you later," Marcus managed to stutter, trying to hide his disappointment.

"Bye," Emma said shortly.

"See you," Ethan added, trying to sound casual.

With that, Sarah turned around and walked away, leaving the trio standing there in silence.

Emma and Ethan exchanged a glance and a small smirk. Marcus knew exactly what they were thinking and rolled his eyes, "Oh shut up, you two." Emma's expression turned serious, "I still don't trust her, Doug's sense of smell couldn't be wrong. He said he smelled that scent before and it was coming from her. But she had a point about the venom being similar to that of a snake. Maybe Jack is the culprit."

Ethan stood there, deep in thought as Emma and Marcus continued to argue back and forth about Sarah's involvement

95

in the case. He had a feeling of uncertainty about the whole situation.

"Come on, Em," Marcus defended Sarah, "think about it. She wasn't at the welcoming speech. And hello?! Snake venom? It all points to Jack."

"But what about Doug's smell?" Emma counters. "He said he recognized that scent from her, and he's never wrong."

"Okay, okay," Ethan interjects, holding up his hands. "Let's not jump to conclusions here. We need to gather more information before we accuse anyone."

Emma and Marcus both turn to look at Ethan, and for a moment the three of them stand in silence, considering the next steps in their investigation.

Finally, Emma nods and says, "Okay, fine. But we need to be careful. We don't want to make the same mistake twice. And, by the way, what's her animal spirit?" Emma asked, trying to steer the conversation back to something concrete.

"Isn't it obvious?" Marcus replied with a grin. "She's super smart and clever, she is a dolphin."

Emma rolled her eyes, and Ethan chuckled, "You really like her, don't you?"

Marcus's face blushed with embarrassment. "I don't know what you're talking about," he mumbled, but his friends knew better.

CHAPTER 12

THINKING AHEAD

After a long and grueling math class, Ethan was feeling relieved to be finished for the day. As he was packing up his things, he felt a tap on his shoulder. When he turned around, he saw Aria standing there, with a mischievous glint in her brown eyes. She was a young Indian-American teen, with long, dark hair that was styled in a sleek ponytail, accentuating her sharp cheekbones and stunning smile. Her golden skin was adorned with a few freckles, adding a touch of warmth to her beauty.

"Hey Ethan, how was math for you today?" Aria asked with a playful tone.

Ethan rolled his eyes, "Don't even get me started, I hate math."

Aria chuckled, "I know, right? But hey, do you want to play a game of chess with me to help get your mind off of it?"

Ethan's eyes lit up at the suggestion, "Sure, I'd love to."

The two of them walked over to one of the tables, and took their seats across from each other. Aria moved the pieces around, setting up the board.

As they started to play, the two of them fell into a comfortable silence, only interrupted by the sound of the pieces moving on the board. Aria was a fierce competitor, but Ethan was able to hold his own. They were evenly matched, and the game was highly entertaining.

Aria's cat-like grace was evident even as she pondered her next move. As she made her selection, she glanced up at Ethan and asked, "So, how's it going here at the Sanctuary? Do you like it?"

Ethan sighed. "I love it, but math class is a real drag."

Aria chuckled. "I know, but we still need to learn all the normal human stuff. At least we get to have Animalian classes, right?"

Ethan nodded, a smile spreading across his face. "Yeah, that's what makes it all worth it. I'm just so excited to be in the Animalian world for the first time."

Aria's eyes widened in surprise. "Really? Your parents aren't Animalians?"

Ethan shook his head. "Nope, I'm a bit of a rarity in that sense."

Aria smiled. "Me too. This is my first time as well, and you're the first person I've met like me."

Ethan leaned back in his chair and grinned. "Looks like we're in this together, then."

The sound of the rook being moved echoed through the quiet room. Aria was about to make her next move when Ethan spoke up.

"So, how did you end up discovering the Animalian world?" Ethan asked.

Aria's hand hovered over the pawn she was about to move. She looked up at Ethan and a small smile played on her lips. "I was just walking home from school one day and a stray cat approached me. It was a black and white cat with green eyes, it was beautiful. The cat started talking to me, can you believe it? It told me about a place where I could learn more about my Animalian abilities, and that's how I was introduced to the Sanctuary and Ms. Rodriguez. She was the one that convinced my parents."

Ethan was amazed. "I had no idea that animals could communicate with us before coming here," he said.

Aria nodded. "I was just as shocked as you. But the cat was so kind and insistent that I listen, and I'm glad I did. I learned so much about myself and my abilities since then."

Ethan leaned back in his chair and crossed his arms. "I was actually contacted and invited by Mr. Black," he said.

Aria leaned forward in her chair, her eyes fixed on the chess board. "Have you heard about the animal poisonings?" she suddenly asked Ethan, changing the subject.

Ethan looked up from the board and nodded. "Well, I actually was there when both happened," he said, his voice tinged with concern.

Aria's eyes widened in surprise. "Ah... should I be afraid?" she asked with a hint of irony.

Ethan chuckled. "Haha, it was just a coincidence. I hope...," he said, trying to lighten the mood.

Aria was still serious, though. "What do you think is going on?" she asked.

"I don't know... maybe someone around here doesn't like animals? That would be ironic," Ethan replied, his brow furrowed in thought.

"Do you think we're in danger?" Aria asked, her tone more serious now.

"I don't think so. Nothing indicates an attack on the people, but even if they continue to attack only animals, that's already bad enough," Ethan replied, his tone reflecting his concern.

Aria nodded in agreement. "Yeah... I hope they figure out what's happening soon."

Ethan sighed. "We actually were following a couple of leads, but they ended up making us more confused," he said, shaking his head.

Aria's eyebrows rose in surprise. "How so?" she asked.

"Well, the leads pointed us to two different persons who claimed they were not where they were allegedly supposed to be," Ethan said, frustration clear in his voice.

Aria leaned back in her chair and thought for a moment. "Maybe they're lying," she said finally.

Ethan nodded. "Yeah, maybe... we need more information," he said, returning his focus to the chess board.

Suddenly, Aria called out, "Checkmate!"

Ethan's eyes widened in surprise. "Hey! Not fair, you were distracting me," he said with a laugh.

Aria smiled. "Well, it's not my fault you couldn't keep up," she teased.

Ethan nodded, "Well, I guess I'll have to come back and get revenge sometime."

Aria playfully rolled her eyes, "Anytime, Ethan. I'll be ready for you," she provoked. "Hey, have you heard about the camping trip we have planned for next week?" Aria asked, her voice filled with excitement.

"Yeah! I'm thrilled about it. I've always wanted to go camping, but my parents never took me," Ethan replied.

"It's going to be such a blast, but there better be s'mores!," Aria emphasized.

"Definitely! I mean, what's a camping trip without s'mores? That's one thing I know from the movies," Ethan stated with a chuckle.

The two of them packed up the pieces, and said their goodbyes, feeling grateful for the unexpected break from their normal routine. They went their separate ways, both looking forward to their next chess match.

CHAPTER 13

UNCOVERING THE TRUTH

On a Saturday morning, Ethan walks through the winding paths of the Sanctuary, camera in hand and a sense of purpose in his step. He stops in a large open field, and looks up to the sky. He takes a deep breath and calls out, "Talon!"

Moments later, a majestic falcon swoops down and lands gracefully on Ethan's outstretched arm. "Hey buddy," Ethan says, affectionately stroking the bird's feathers.

The two spend some time together, with Ethan taking pictures and talking to Talon. He tells him about his worries and frustrations with the ongoing investigation, and Talon listens attentively. As they talk, Ethan finds a state of clarity and understanding that he can't find anywhere else.

"Thanks Talon, you always know how to put things in perspective for me," Ethan says as he watches the bird take flight. He feels a sensation of peace and renewed determination as he continues his walk, ready to tackle whatever challenges come his way.

As Ethan walked past Ms. Park's office, he couldn't help but notice that the door was slightly ajar. He couldn't see much from the doorway, but he could tell that something was off. He couldn't quite put his finger on it, but he felt compelled to investigate. As he approached the door, he called out to Ms. Park, but there was no response. He pushed the door open a little further and peered inside. What he saw made his heart race. Ms. Park was sitting in her chair, her head slumped over her desk. She was completely unconscious.

Ethan quickly realized that something was seriously wrong. He rushed over to Ms. Park and shook her gently, trying to rouse her, but she didn't respond. He noticed a pencil lying on the desk next to her and a piece of paper with "Leo." written on it. Suddenly, he heard the sound of Braveheart's voice coming from down the hall, talking to another teacher. Ethan knew he had to act fast. He grabbed the piece of paper and quickly hid it in his pocket.

Just as he was about   to leave the office, the door opened in front of him. It was Braveheart and another teacher. Braveheart saw Ethan standing there, looking guilty, and immediately knew something was wrong. He rushed over to Ms. Park, checked her pulse, and then turned to Ethan. "What happened here? What are you doing in Ms. Park's office?"

Ethan's mind was racing. He didn't know what to say. He had been caught red-handed, and he knew he couldn't just come up with a good excuse on the spot. All he could think about was the piece of paper in his pocket and what it could mean. He could see the suspicion in Braveheart's eyes and knew he had to come up with something fast.

Ethan knew he had to come clean, but he also couldn't reveal everything. "I-I don't know," he stammered. "I just saw the door open and wanted to check on her. I didn't see anything else, I swear."

The other teacher, a young woman with short blonde hair, was looking around the room, trying to figure out what was going on. She noticed a cup of tea on the desk, still steaming, and a notebook open next to it. She picked up the notebook and started flipping through the pages. "This is Ms. Park's lesson plan for today," she said. "She must have been working on it before something happened."

Braveheart picked Ms. Park up in his arms and carried her to the infirmary. Braveheart turned to Ethan and said, "I expect you to come up to my office this afternoon, we need to have a talk."

Ethan rushed back to the dormitory, his mind racing with thoughts of what had just happened in Ms. Park's office. He knew he needed to talk to Marcus and Emma, but first he had to find them. He searched the common areas of the dormitory, but they were nowhere to be found. He started to feel a sense of panic rising in his chest.

He finally found Marcus in his dorm room, lying on his bed and taking a nap. Ethan tried to shake him awake, but he was groggy and slow to respond. "Marcus, wake up," Ethan said urgently. "I need to talk to you and Emma." He pulled him out of bed and the two of them set off to find Emma.

When they finally found Emma, she was sitting in the library, lost in a book. Ethan pulled her away from her studies, and the three of them sat down in a quiet corner. Emma looked at Ethan expectantly, "What's going on?" she asked.

Ethan took a deep breath before he began to explain. "I just found Ms. Park unconscious in her office. I don't know what happened, but something is really wrong. And I found this," he said as he pulled the piece of paper out of his pocket and handed it to Emma. She looked at it and read the name "Leo" aloud.

Marcus's eyes went wide. "Leo Braveheart?" he exclaimed. "Do you think he had something to do with this?"

Ethan shook his head. "I don't know, but why would Ms. Park write Leo Braveheart's name on this piece of paper?"

Emma's eyes widened as she looked at the paper. "So it was Braveheart who was responsible for all the poisonings," she said, her voice barely above a whisper.

Ethan looked at Emma, a deep frown etched into his forehead. "It's hard to believe," he said. "But appearances can be deceiving."

Marcus leaned forward, his expression serious. "Even though Braveheart seems to be a good man, I've heard some creepy stories about him," he said. "Like the time he was chasing this criminal and instead of capturing him, he let him fall into a crocodile den. The only thing that was left of the guy was one leg."

Emma and Ethan looked at each other, their expressions a mix of shock and disbelief.

Emma looked at the paper and then back at Ethan. "Why didn't you show this to the teachers?" she asked.

Ethan hung his head, feeling guilty. "I panicked," he said. "I didn't know what to do."

Ethan looked at Emma and Marcus with a sense of unease. "Braveheart wants to talk to me," he said.

Emma's face immediately twisted with concern. "You can't go, Ethan," she said, her voice filled with urgency. "It's not safe."

Ethan shook his head. "I don't think Braveheart is aware that we know anything," he said. "I might be able to get more information if I go."

Marcus nodded in agreement. "He's right, Emma," he said. "It will look suspicious if he doesn't show up. We need to know what's really going on."

Ethan took a deep breath and tried to steady his nerves. He knew that this was a risky move, but he couldn't shake the feeling that he needed to do this. He couldn't just sit back and wait for things to happen. He had to be proactive and try to uncover the truth.

Ethan attempted to ease the tension with a playful comment. "I'll be sure to keep an eye out for any suspicious snacks from Braveheart. And if anything happens to me, you'll know for certain he's behind it."

Emma and Marcus didn't seem amused. Emma shook her head. "This isn't a joke, Ethan. This is serious. You need to be careful."

Ethan knew she was right, but he didn't want to let on that he was scared. "I'll be fine," he said. "I'll just play it cool and see if I can get any more information out of him."

Marcus nodded. "Just be careful, Ethan. And if anything seems off, get out of there as fast as you can."

Ethan took a deep breath and tried to steady himself. He knew this was a risky move, but he had a feeling like it was the only way to get to the bottom of what was happening at the Sanctuary. "I'll take care," he said. "Don't worry, I'll be back soon."

With that, Ethan set off to meet with Braveheart, trying to keep a brave face and not let on how scared he was feeling inside. He didn't know what to expect, but he knew he had to be ready for anything.

As Ethan walked into the main administrative building of the Sanctuary, memories of his previous visits to Braveheart's office flooded back to him. The grand foyer with its high ceiling and marble flooring, the paintings and tapestries adorning the walls, the statues and sculptures on display, and the soft classical music filling the air all reminded him of the grandeur and sophistication of the place. He approached the reception desk, where a woman in a smart business suit sat, and announced his presence to see the headmaster.

As he was led to the office, Ethan felt uneasy. He remembered the last time he was here, and how Braveheart had questioned him about the series of strange occurrences at the Sanctuary. He couldn't shake off the feeling that the headmaster suspected him of something.

When he entered the office, Braveheart was sitting behind a large, imposing desk, his cold, piercing blue eyes staring at Ethan intently. He was an imposing figure, tall and broad-shouldered, with short, gray hair and a stern expression. He was dressed in a tailored suit, and his presence commanded attention.

Braveheart gestured for Ethan to take a seat in front of the desk, and then leaned forward, his gaze never leaving Ethan's face. "Explain to me what happened in Ms. Park's office," he said in a cold, demanding tone.

Ethan took a deep breath and tried to steady himself. He explained what had happened in Ms. Park's office, how he had found her unconscious and how he had called for help. He didn't mention the piece of paper with "Leo." written on it.

Braveheart listened to Ethan's explanation, his expression impassive. When Ethan finished, Braveheart leaned back in his chair and looked at him thoughtfully. "I don't know why you are always present when these things happen, Ethan," he said. "It could just be coincidence, but I would advise you to be careful."

Ethan felt a chill run down his spine. Braveheart's words were not a threat, but they were certainly not a reassurance either. He mustered up the courage to inquire, "Sir, have there been any developments in the search for a cure or in identifying the individual responsible for the poisonings?"

Braveheart's expression was grave as he replied, "I regret to inform you that our search for a cure remains fruitless and our investigations are still ongoing. But I must emphasize the gravity of the situation. If we do not swiftly bring this to an end, the school will no longer be a safe environment for our students."

Ethan nods understandingly and Braveheart dismisses him, and Ethan left the office with a heavy heart, unsure of what the future holds for the Sanctuary. He couldn't shake off the feeling that Braveheart knew more than he was letting on.

As Ethan emerged from the main administrative building, Marcus and Emma were waiting for him outside. They both looked at him with worried expressions on their faces.

"So, how did it go?" Emma asked, her voice laced with concern.

Ethan let out a sigh. "It was... uncomfortable," he said. "Braveheart was asking a lot of questions about what happened in Ms. Park's office, and I could tell he was trying to gauge my reaction. Also, Braveheart still has no leads on the cure or the culprit, or at least, none that he was willing to share with me."

Marcus furrowed his brow. "Did he say anything about the paper with 'Leo' on it?"

Ethan shook his head. "No, and I didn't mention it. I didn't want to tip him off that we know something."

Emma nodded, her expression thoughtful. "That's probably for the best. We need to be careful about what we say and to whom."

Marcus nodded in agreement. "Yeah, and we need to figure out what that paper means. I have a bad feeling about this whole thing."

Emma looked worried. "What are we going to do?"

"I think we should talk to Mr. Black about it," Ethan said thoughtfully. "I trust him and I believe he could be a valuable asset in a confrontation against Braveheart."

"I agree," Marcus chimed in. "Mr. Black has always been fair to us and I think he would be willing to help."

Emma nodded in agreement. "It's definitely worth a shot. Plus, we should check on him anyway to see how he's doing. I heard that Mr. Black and Ms. Park used to be in a relationship in the past."

CHAPTER 14

THE HUNT FOR A SUSPECT

The next morning, Ethan, Emma, and Marcus made their way to Combat Training class with Mr. Black. Even though Marcus wasn't officially part of that class, he decided to come along and participate in the conversation with Mr. Black.

As they entered the training room, they saw Mr. Black already there, setting up equipment for the class. "Good morning, Mr. Black," Emma greeted him cheerfully.

Mr. Black turned around and smiled, "Good morning, students. What can I do for you?"

Ethan stepped forward, "We wanted to talk to you about something. We were wondering if we could have a word with you?"

Mr. Black's expression turned serious, "I see. Unfortunately, I cannot talk to you right now. I must start class, but I can give you a few minutes after class ends."

Marcus let out a sigh, "Well, I guess we'll have to wait then."

Ethan and Emma nodded and took their places in the class, but Marcus decided to sit on the side and wait, reading a book. Emma noticed this and said, "Hey Marcus, why don't you join the class today? It's always good to improve your combat skills."

But Marcus shook his head and replied, "No thanks, Emma. I'm more of a book-smart person than a brawn-smart person. I'll stick to reading and strategizing, while you guys do the fighting."

Ethan laughed and said, "Yeah, Marcus likes to leave the physical work to us. He's the brains of the operation, while we're the muscles."

Marcus grinned and rolled his eyes playfully, "I'll stick to that, thank you very much."

"Hey Ethan," Alex greeted him with a smile. "Do you want to pair up again today?"

Ethan chuckled and replied, "Sorry buddy, but I think I'll find someone with a similar strength this time. How about you pair up with Emma?" He gestured towards Emma who was standing nearby.

Emma smiled and nodded, "Sure, sounds good to me."

Alex's face fell slightly at Ethan's rejection, but he quickly recovered and agreed to the new pairing. "Sure, no problem. I'll work on holding back a bit," he said with a chuckle.

Ethan knew that Alex's small size belied his true strength, as his animal spirit was that of an ant. He had found out the hard way that Alex was incredibly strong and it was taking a toll on his body. He didn't want to deal with that again today, but he knew that Alex meant well and didn't want to hurt his feelings.

As the class began, Ethan watched as they worked together, it was intriguing to see Emma's bear power match up against Alex's ant strength. He couldn't help but feel a twinge of jealousy, wishing he could have a partner like Emma in his own training. But he pushed the feeling aside and focused on his own training.

Ethan was stretching and warming up when Isabella approaches him with a smile on her face. She has dark hair that falls in loose waves down her back, framing her tanned face. Her sharp cheekbones and strong jawline are accentuated by her freckles, which dot her nose and cheeks. Isabella is lean and athletic, and you can see the muscles in her arms and legs tense as she moves with fluid grace.

"Hey Ethan," Isabella says, her voice light and friendly. "Do you want to pair up for today's practice?"

Ethan looks up and nods, impressed by Isabella's confidence. As they stepped onto the training field, Mr. Black barked out instructions.

"Alright students, today we will be practicing hand-to-hand combat. You will be paired up, and your partner will be your opponent. I want to see what you've learned so far, and see how you work together in a fight. Remember, this is all just training, so don't hold back."

Isabella stepped forward, a confident smile on her face. Her dark hair was pulled back into a high ponytail, revealing her freckled face. She was a jaguar Animalian, and her spirit animal shimmered just beneath the surface, giving her a lithe, powerful presence.

Ethan stood across from her, trying to hide his nerves. He knew he was no match for Isabella, who was known for her capoeira fighting style. He had seen her practicing before, and her fluid movements were nothing short of awe-inspiring.

The two of them took their positions, and Mr. Black signaled for them to begin. Isabella didn't waste any time, launching into a series of graceful kicks and spins. Ethan tried his best to block her attacks, but she was too fast.

"C'mon Ethan, keep up!" Isabella taunted, a teasing smile on her face.

"You're pretty fast," Ethan says, catching his breath.

She effortlessly performed the au, the capoeira cartwheel, as she dodged Ethan's strikes. Ethan was taken aback by her grace and finesse, having never seen anyone fight like this before.

Isabella then sprang into action, unleashing a flurry of strikes, combining her jaguar speed with her capoeira techniques. Ethan found himself struggling to keep up with her, as she moved with the fluidity of water, always adapting to his movements.

The two of them continued to fight, both learning from each other, until Isabella performed a stunning backflip, landing gracefully in front of Ethan, followed by a sweep kick. She smiled and extended a hand, helping Ethan back up to his feet.

"You're getting better, Ethan," Isabella said with a grin. "But don't let your guard down, I'm sure you'll beat me one day."

Ethan laughed and nodded, impressed by Isabella's skills and determination. He was grateful for the chance to practice with her and was excited to see what other skills she could bring to the training ground.

Ethan, Marcus, and Emma waited for all the students to leave before approaching Mr. Black. "How are you holding up?" Ethan asked, concern etched on his face.

Mr. Black let out a sigh. "Ms. Park is a dear friend, so it's been hard, but I'm determined to put an end to this."

Ethan nodded, understanding all too well the feeling of wanting to solve a mystery. "I know you're aware I was the one who found her unconscious," Ethan said, "I can tell you everything that happened in detail if you'd like."

Mr. Black nods, "Yes please, any information can help in finding out what happened to Ms. Park."

Ethan recounted the details of that day, describing how he found Ms. Park unconscious at her desk, and how he had tried to rouse her but was unsuccessful. "Then, I found this lying next to her," Ethan said.

As Ethan pulled out the piece of paper from his pocket and handed it to Mr. Black, the older man's expression turned to one of confusion and concern. "Leo... hm... it can't be."

Emma spoke up hesitantly, "Mr. Black, we believe Leo Braveheart might be behind the poisonings."

Mr. Black looked at Emma, his expression unreadable. He was silent for a moment, lost in thought. Marcus tried to speak up, but Mr. Black cut him off. "What? Braveheart? I trust Braveheart completely. He would never hurt Ms. Park or any of the animals. He wouldn't be capable of something like this."

Marcus, who had been standing silently next to Emma, spoke up. "But Mr. Black, the evidence-"

Mr. Black cut him off, his voice firm. "I understand your concerns, but I trust Leo completely. I refuse to believe that he would do something like this."

The three students exchanged glances, unsure of what to say. Mr. Black stood up from his desk and walked towards the door. "I must go. I will talk to you all later."

With that, Mr. Black left the room, leaving the three students standing there, unsure of what to do next. They couldn't shake the feeling that there was more to the story than what met the eye. And now, with Mr. Black's reluctance to entertain their suspicions, they were left to wonder if they were on the right path or not.

Emma let out a frustrated sigh, "Ugh, why does this have to be so confusing? We have clues pointing to Jack, clues pointing to Sarah, and the strongest clue pointing to Braveheart, but none of it fits together."

Ethan nodded, "Yeah, it's like trying to solve a jigsaw puzzle with missing pieces."

"We need more information. We have to keep digging, keep piecing together the clues," Marcus replied.

"But what if we're wrong?" Emma asked, her voice laced with uncertainty.

"We have to be sure," Ethan replied. "We can't jump to conclusions. We need to keep an open mind and explore all the possibilities."

Emma let out a sigh. "I just wish there was a way to know for sure."

Ethan nodded. "I know, but we have to trust our instincts and our research. We'll figure it out. We just have to be patient."

"I hope you're right, but I don't know how much time we got before things go from bad to worse," Emma said, her voice shaking with worry.

CHAPTER 15

THE FALLS OF THE MOON

The sun was shining bright and the birds were singing, the perfect day for a field trip. This weekend, the students in Ethan's grade were about to go on a hiking and camping trip to a nearby waterfall. Ethan rubbed his eyes, trying to shake off the last bits of sleep as he sat up in his bed. He looked around at Marcus, who were still soundly sleeping, and slipped out of bed, feeling excited for the day ahead. He grabbed his backpack, which was already packed with supplies for the camping trip, and approached his friend.

Marcus was still groggy, trying to shield his eyes from the bright sun, as Ethan came close. "Morning Marcus," Ethan said with a grin, trying to get the grumpy owl Animalian in a better mood. Marcus grumbled a response, which Ethan took as a good sign. He wasn't a morning person, especially since his talents were more attuned to the night.

"You ready for this?" Ethan asked, looking over the list of supplies they had to bring with them. Marcus nodded, but didn't say anything.

Ethan and Marcus made their way to the cafeteria for a quick breakfast before the camping trip. Emma had already beaten them there and was waiting for them at a table with a steaming cup of coffee and a plate of eggs and toast.

"Good morning, guys!" Emma greeted cheerfully as Ethan and Marcus approached the table.

Marcus groaned and rubbed his eyes, still feeling the effects of waking up in the bright sun. "I don't know how you can be so cheerful this early," he grumbled, taking a seat across from Emma.

"Come on, Marcus, it's a beautiful day! And we get to spend it camping and hiking at the waterfall!" Ethan said excitedly, grabbing a plate and piling it high with pancakes.

Emma smiled at Ethan's enthusiasm and then turned to Marcus. "What do you think about the waterfall? I heard it has a special name."

"Oh yeah, it's called the 'Falls of the Moon'," Marcus said, finally starting to perk up. "There's a legend that says it was formed from a single tear of the moon goddess. She was said to have been so overwhelmed by the beauty of the world that she cried a single tear that flowed down to the earth and formed the waterfall."

Ethan listened intently to the legend, his eyes wide with wonder. "Wow, that's a cool story! I can't wait to see it."

Emma nodded in agreement, taking a sip of her coffee. "Me too. I heard it's a pretty challenging hike, but the view is worth it."

Marcus grumbled under his breath about the upcoming hike. "I don't understand why we have to walk all the way to the Falls of the Moon," he muttered to Ethan and Emma. "Can't we just fly there or something?"

Emma chuckled and rolled his eyes. "I heard it's even more beautiful during a full moon, which just so happens to be this weekend."

Marcus brightened up at that news. "Really? A full moon? That's perfect! Owls are especially powerful under the light of the moon."

Ethan, Emma, and Marcus gathered their gear for the camping hike and joined other students outside the main building. Isabella, Aria, Michael, Jack, and several other students from their grade were already there. As they gathered, Isabella approached Ethan and his friends, her toned muscles rippling like a big feline.

"Hey guys," she said with a confident smile. "Ready for this hike?"

"You know it," replied Ethan, adjusting his backpack. "I can't wait to get out into nature and explore."

"Same here," chimed in Emma, who was always eager for adventure. "I've heard the views from the top of the mountain are incredible."

Marcus nodded in agreement, but added, "Just as long as we don't run into any dangerous beasts. This forest can be pretty wild."

Isabella laughed, her golden eyes shining. "Don't worry, Marcus. I'll protect you all with my capoeira skills."

The group laughed. As they gathered near the entrance to the woods, the sound of rapid footsteps echoed through the clearing. Alex stumbled into view, panting and sweating profusely. "I'm so sorry, I got held up at the last minute," he panted, trying to catch his breath.

As Alex rushed to catch up with the rest of the group, the Stone brothers snickered to each other. "Looks like someone overslept," Jake teased.

Mr. Black, the group's supervisor, placed a hand on Alex's shoulder. "It's alright, take a moment to catch your breath." The group had gathered around, watching as Mr. Black gave a rousing speech. "Today, we embark on a journey. A journey of discovery and growth. Remember, we're all in this together, and the most important thing is to have each other's backs. We will be hiking to the nearby waterfall and setting up camp there. It will take us about four hours to reach the destination, so make sure you are properly equipped and have enough food and water with you."

With the pep talk over, the group started the walk towards their camping site. Ethan and his friends Emma and Marcus walked together, chatting and laughing as they made their way through the forest.

As they continued on their journey, the group found themselves surrounded by towering trees and lush greenery. The chirping of birds and the rustling of leaves filled the air, and the scent of pine and earth wafted around them. The forest was alive with activity as creatures big and small scurried about.

Ethan marveled at the beauty of the forest as they hiked. He noticed the way the sunlight filtered through the leaves, casting a dappled pattern on the ground. A family of deer grazed nearby, completely unbothered by the group's presence. The underbrush was alive with the colorful flutter of butterflies, and the distant calls of unfamiliar animals echoed through the trees. Ethan felt as though he had stepped into another world, one where nature was still king and the creatures of the forest roamed free.

As the group continued their hike through the lush forest, Aria suddenly spoke up. "You know, I'm just fascinated by how they keep the Animalian world hidden from the rest of humanity. How does that even work?"

Marcus, who was walking beside her, chuckled. "Okay, so here's the deal," he began, a grin spreading across his face as he savored the opportunity to share his knowledge. "It's not magic that keep us hidden from humans. It's actually a combination of things."

"There's us, the Animalians. We're trained from a young age to keep our abilities and identities concealed from humans. We know how to blend in and act like regular humans. Plus, most humans just wouldn't believe that people with super abilities like us even exist."

"And, there's the cooperation between Animalians and humans. The Council of Elders, a group of highly respected and influential Animalians, has established alliances with key figures in the human government and society. They've made sure that only the right people know about us and that any information that could potentially leak is swiftly dealt with. It's a delicate balance, but so far it's been working pretty well."

"So, you see," Marcus concluded with a shrug. "It's not just one thing, but a whole system that keeps us hidden. And I gotta say, it's pretty cool that we get to be part of this secret world."

Ethan rubbed his chin thoughtfully as they walked through the forest. "But why humans help keep the

Animalian world a secret?" He said. "What do they get out of it?"

Marcus, who had always been interested in the history and politics of the Animalian world, was ready with an answer. "There are a few reasons," he began. "One of the main ones is to avoid a war. If the rest of humanity found out about us, there could be mass panic and chaos. It could also lead to conflicts and wars between different nations who would want to control us and use our powers for their own purposes. Also, they get access to our skills and abilities," Marcus said. "Animalians are highly advanced in many areas, such as technology, medicine, and the arts. By working together with us, they can benefit from our expertise. For example, did you know that Einstein was actually a genius dolphin Animalian?"

Emma's eyes widened in surprise. "No way! I had no idea."

"Yep, it's true," Marcus confirmed with a nod. "There are many famous people throughout history who were actually Animalians, and their powers and abilities were kept hidden from the rest of the world. By working together with us, humans can gain access to our knowledge and skills, and the world benefits from their advancements."

As they continued their conversation, Jack joined in, having listened to their discussion from a distance. He leaned against a tree, arms crossed, and interjected, "I disagree. Animalians are stronger, faster, smarter, and better in every way. We should be leading society, not hiding from it."

The others gasped in shock at Jack's statement. Isabella stepped forward, her eyes blazing with anger. "That is a dangerous and cruel mentality, Jack," she said firmly. "Animalians and humans coexist for a reason. We share this world and must learn to live in harmony, not one species ruling over the other. That kind of thinking leads to nothing but conflict and destruction."

Emma nodded in agreement, adding, "Besides, it's not just about physical strength. Humans have their own unique skills and qualities that are just as important. It's not a matter of one being better than the other."

Ethan listened carefully to the conversation, considering the different perspectives. He was grateful for friends who were always willing to engage in thoughtful discussions and consider all sides of an issue.

As Jack continued to argue his point, the rest of the group grew increasingly agitated. "You can have your opinion, but you can't deny the facts," Jack said defiantly. "Animalians are better in every way. It's just survival of the fittest. Sooner or later, we're going to rule the world."

Emma, who had been listening patiently, finally cracked her knuckles as she stepped forward. "Well, if that's the case, then I should 'rule' you," she said, her voice strong and confident. "I'm stronger, so why not?"

The group fell silent, taken aback by Emma's bold statement. Jack's eyes widened as he looked at Emma, fear evident in his expression. He took a step back, nearly tripping over a tree root in his haste to get away from the young, fiery fawn. "Whoa, okay there. I didn't mean to offend anyone. Let's just calm down and enjoy the hike," Jack stammered, trying to diffuse the tension.

Jack swallowed hard, his eyes darting from Emma to the other students around them. He could see the disapproval in their eyes, and he knew that he had gone too far.

As the tension in the air began to thicken, Marcus stepped forward, a wide grin spreading across his face. "Well, I think it's safe to say that none of us want to get on Emma's bad side," he said, trying to ease the tension. "I mean, those knuckles of hers could probably crush a coconut with one squeeze."

Everyone chuckled, the sound of their laughter breaking the tension and restoring the group's good mood. Alex even let out a sigh of relief, happy that the focus was no longer on his tardiness or Jack's controversial opinions.

Isabella smiled, glad to see that the group was back to their light-hearted selves. "Come on, let's keep moving," she said, gesturing for them to continue down the trail. "The forest is filled with so much more to discover, and I for one am not about to miss out on the chance to see all its wonders." Her jaguar spirit eager to explore the wildness.

The group of teenagers took a break on a green hill surrounded by towering trees. They took out their backpacks and pulled out snacks and drinks, settling into a circle on the grass. Mr. Black, who had been leading the hike, took a seat next to Ethan, Emma, and Aria. He leaned back, crossing his legs at the ankles, and gazed out at the scenery.

"This place is special," Mr. Black began, his voice low and melodic. "It's called the Enchanted Forest, and it's said to be enchanted by the fairies who once lived here. They were mischievous creatures, but they were also kind and generous. They would grant wishes to travelers who passed through the forest, but only if they showed respect for the land and its creatures."

The students listened in awe as Mr. Black continued his story. "One day, a group of humans came through the forest, hunting for the fairies. They wanted to capture them and sell them as pets. The fairies were furious, and they punished the humans by casting a spell that made them forget about the fairies and the magic of the forest."

Mr. Black paused, looking around at the students. "And that's why this forest is still here, hidden from the rest of the world. The fairies' magic protects it, and it's still a place of wonder and magic. If you're lucky, you might see a glimpse of a fairy, but you must be careful not to disturb them."

The students sat in silence, absorbing Mr. Black's story. They were captivated by the thought of a hidden, enchanted forest, and they all felt a sense of wonder and magic as they looked around at their surroundings.

"Come on, Mr. Black," Tyler, one of the Stone brothers, interjected, "Do you really expect us to believe in this fairy tale you're telling us?"

Mr. Black chuckled and replied, "I understand your skepticism, Tyler. But I can assure you, this is not just a story. This place holds a rich history and special energy that can be felt by those who are open to it."

"AHHH! Get it off!" Aria screeched, jumping up from her spot on the ground. Zack, the youngest of the three, with a smirk on his face, had reached over to touch Aria's ankle with a spiky plant, pretending it was a bug.

"Relax, Aria," Zack chuckled, "It's just a plant. Or is it?" He wiggled his eyebrows, trying to scare her further. But Aria wasn't having it. She stepped the plant down like a cat saying "Knock it off!" The group burst into laughter, the previously tense atmosphere dissolving in the lighthearted moment.

As the group continued on their hike, the scenery around them began to change. The lush green trees grew taller and the ground became more rocky and uneven. The river that flowed beside them was now wider and more powerful, the sound of rushing water filling the air. A gentle breeze blew through the area, carrying the scent of pine and damp earth.

Marcus was beginning to struggle with his heavy pack, and his steps were slowing down. "This hike is never-ending," he grumbled. "I'm so tired."

That's when Alex stepped forward, offering to help. "I've got you, man," he said, hefting Marcus's pack with ease. Despite his slender build, Alex's ant-like strength was impressive.

Ethan chuckled as he watched, always amused by the sight of such a thin boy being able to carry so much weight. "You never cease to amaze me, Alex," he said.

As the group hiked further up the river, the sound of rushing water grew louder and louder until finally, they reached the Falls of the Moon. The waterfall was a magnificent sight, cascading down in a shimmering silver sheet from a height that seemed to touch the sky. The sun was starting to set, casting an orange-pink hue over the surrounding trees, making the waterfall's mist glow in an ethereal light. The river widened at the base of the waterfall, creating a tranquil pool that sparkled like a thousand diamonds. The group stood in awe, taking in the breathtaking beauty of the Falls of the Moon. "Wow," whispered Isabella, her eyes shining with wonder. "This is... incredible."

Marcus approached the edge of the pool, dipping his hand into the water. "It's ice cold," he said, shivering.

"Let's set up camp here," said Mr. Black, smiling at the group's reactions. "We'll have a fire and make dinner, then rest for the night. We have a big day ahead of us tomorrow." The group nodded in agreement, and set about setting up camp at the base of the Falls of the Moon.

As the sun continue to set, casting a warm glow over the forest, Ethan, Marcus, and Alex struggled to put up their tent, until Isabella stepped in to help.

"I've been camping since I was a kid," she said, deftly tying the ropes and securing the tent. "It's a family tradition. My dad used to take us camping every summer."

Once the tents were set up, Mr. Black approached them, clapping his hands. "Alright, kids! You've done a great job setting up. Now, go ahead and explore a bit. Let your inner animals come out. But remember, it'll be dark soon so don't go too far," he said, smiling.

The students cheered and scattered in different directions, eager to explore their surroundings. The students were finally able to let loose after a long day of hiking. Some of them were running around, jumping from rock to rock, and climbing trees with ease. Others were a bit more reserved, preferring to sit and take in their surroundings. But, regardless of their activity level, the group's Animalian abilities were on full display.

Isabella, with her graceful movements, jumped from rock to rock like a jaguar. It was a sight to behold. Emma, with her immense strength, was playing a game of catch with Alex, tossing a large boulder back and forth. They made it look like child's play.

Ethan climbed a hill and stood atop of it, taking in the breathtaking view of the mountains and verdant forests that surrounded them. The peaceful sound of the nearby waterfall and the cool breeze blowing through the trees made him feel as if he was in a different world. As he gazed out at the scenery, an inexplicable urge rose within him, an urge to spread his wings and soar above it all.

He took a step forward, his foot hovering over the edge of the cliff. The wind gusted, lifting his hair, and he felt as if he was already flying. Suddenly, a voice called out to him, breaking the spell.

"Ethan! Get down from there, man. We need to get back to camp." It was Marcus, making his way up the hill towards him.

Ethan turned to look at Marcus, frustration evident in his eyes. "What's the hurry?" he asked.

"Mr. Black wants us back at camp. Dinner is almost ready and he wants to go over the plans for tomorrow," Marcus replied, still not noticing the inner turmoil Ethan was experiencing.

Ethan sighed and reluctantly stepped back from the edge, feeling a sense of disappointment. He followed Marcus back down the hill towards camp, trying to shake off the feeling of longing. As they walked, he couldn't help but wonder what would have happened if Marcus hadn't interrupted him.

Once they arrived back at camp, the group settled around the fire and began eating their dinner, chatting and laughing together. Their faces lit up by the warm orange light as they took in the beauty of the Falls of the Moon. The waterfall was a breathtaking sight, the water cascading down in a never-ending stream, reflecting the light of the full moon overhead. The full moon was so bright it was as if it was day, the light it cast gave everything an almost surreal quality.

As they sat there, Mr. Black began to tell a story, his voice low and ominous. "Have you all heard the tale of the Falls of the Moon?" he asked, his eyes gleaming in the firelight. The students all nodded, eager to hear what he had to say.

"Long ago, this place was said to be cursed by a powerful sorceress. The sorceress was said to be so beautiful that the moon itself was envious of her and so, in a fit of rage, the moon turned her into stone." Mr. Black's voice was filled with drama and the students were entranced by his words.

"But her curse didn't end there," he continued. "It was said that on every full moon, she would come back to life and terrorize anyone who dared to camp near the waterfall. And the only way to break the curse was to perform a ritual beneath the full moon, but nobody has ever been brave enough to attempt it."

The students all shivered, looking around nervously as the wind picked up and the leaves rustled in the trees. Mr. Black paused for a moment, then continued in a voice filled with mock horror, "But beware, for if you hear the sound of the sorceress' laughter, it is already too late. She has come for you."

Just then, a distant howl echoed through the forest, causing the students to jump in their seats. They all burst into laughter. The Stone brothers could not resist and started howling to the full moon too.

Ethan took a deep breath, savoring the crisp, cool air of the forest. He looked around at the group, still huddled around the campfire, and felt a sense of belonging. Despite their diverse personalities, they all shared a common bond – their animal abilities. And as he gazed into the warm flames, he felt like he had finally found his place in the world.

"You know, I never felt like I fit in before," he said to Marcus, who was sitting next to him. "But now, being here with all of you, it's like I belong."

Marcus nodded, understanding exactly what Ethan meant. "I know what you mean, man," he said. "Being around people who are like us, it's like we don't have to hide who we are."

As the night wore on and the fire died down, the group retired to their tents for the night. Ethan lay in his sleeping bag, listening to the sounds of the forest outside and the soft snores of Michael. Marcus on the other hand, was reading a book in the dark.

CHAPTER 16

BATTLE AT THE MOUNTAINS

Ethan rubbed the sleep from his eyes as he stepped out of the tent and was greeted by the bright light of the morning sun. The chatter of his fellow students filled the air as they went about their morning routines. Marcus, on the other hand, was still fast asleep, snuggled up in his sleeping bag.

As Ethan stumbled out of the tent, he was greeted by Emma, Aria, and Isabella. "Good morning!" they chimed in unison, as they sipped on their morning coffee.

Ethan shyly replied, "Good morning." He ran his fingers through his hair, trying to fix it in a somewhat presentable manner. He looked around and took in the stunning scenery that surrounded them. The river that they had followed yesterday was still flowing peacefully, and the sound of the water was a soothing background noise. The mountains were visible in the distance, and the greenery that surrounded them was a sight to behold. The sun was shining, and the birds were chirping, creating a vibe of calm and peace.

Ethan wandered around the camp, taking in all the sights and sounds around him. He spotted Alex splitting firewood, Michael still snoozing in his tent, and Mr. Black making coffee over the campfire.

As he approached the fire, Mr. Black looked up and smiled. "Good morning, Ethan. Did you have a good sleep?"

"Yes, sir. It was amazing. I've never slept so well," Ethan replied.

"That's what the great outdoors can do for you," Mr. Black said as he handed Ethan a steaming cup of coffee. "Take a seat and enjoy the morning. We have a big day ahead of us."

Ethan grabbed a plate and joined the group, grabbing a sandwich and a cup of coffee. Just then, Alex walked by with a stack of firewood, "Hey guys, want to hear a joke? Why don't scientists trust atoms? Because they make up everything."

The group erupted in laughter, their breakfast interrupted by the silly joke. Marcus, who had just woken up, rubbed his eyes and looked around, "What did I miss?"

"Just Alex's terrible jokes," Aria said, still giggling.

Ethan smiled, feeling grateful to be surrounded by such friendly and lighthearted people. He took another bite of his sandwich and enjoyed the rest of his breakfast, feeling content and at peace.

Later, Mr. Black called for the students attention. "Today, we're going on a hike to the nearby mountain, Mount Mystic, to explore its magnificent peaks and hidden wonders. We'll be leaving soon, so make sure you have plenty of water with you," Mr. Black continued. "We'll be back around noon, in time for lunch and to pack up our things before heading back to the Sanctuary."

Ethan quickly gobbled down the rest of his breakfast, eager to start the day's adventure. He joined the rest of the students as they gathered their supplies and began to make their way towards Mount Mystic.

As they made their way up the mountain, the scenery around them changed dramatically. The lush greenery of the forest gave way to barren rock formations and towering cliffs, and the air grew colder and crisper with each step they took. The students laughter and chatter filled the air. Suddenly, Mr. Black held up a hand, signaling for the students to be quiet. "I think I just heard something," he said, his expression serious. He walked slowly, listening intently to his surroundings.

As Mr. Black cautiously took measured steps, a hush fell over the group, accentuated by the growing tension in the air. Michael started to whisper, "What's going on," but was quickly hushed by Isabella. The only sounds that could be heard were the distant chirps of birds.

Just then, a massive gorilla leaped out from behind a boulder and grabbed Mr. Black in its powerful arms. The students gasped in shock as the two of them engaged in a fierce wrestling match. "Back away!" Mr. Black shouted to the students as he struggled against the gorilla.

With his arms spread wide and his fingers grappling for purchase, the gorilla launched himself at Mr. Black, seeking to overpower the smaller man. He attempted to lift Mr. Black, but the Animalian held his ground, his muscles straining as he pushed back against his opponent. With lightning-fast reflexes, Mr. Black stepped to the side and caught the gorilla off-balance. The gorilla stumbled, and Mr. Black took advantage of the moment.

With a swift and powerful move, he wrapped his arms around the gorilla's neck and began to apply pressure. The gorilla roared in frustration and struggled to break free, but Mr. Black held fast. His muscles bulged as he pulled with all his might, and the gorilla started to gasp for air. But just as it seemed like Mr. Black was about to win the fight, the gorilla found a burst of energy. He shook off Mr. Black's grip and broke free, letting out a triumphant roar.

The students watched in stunned silence as the two figures tumbled and wrestled on the ground. Mr. Black and the gorilla were evenly matched, and neither could gain the upper hand. They rolled and punched and kicked, each trying to get the advantage. The students could barely keep up with the action, and they stood frozen in awe as they watched the two combatants fight to a standstill.

Finally, the gorilla lifted and threw Mr. Black to the ground and raised its fist, ready to strike. But then, to the students' surprise, Mr. Black started to laugh. "You got me, Chico," he said, getting to his feet with the gorilla's help. The gorilla, Chico, let out a friendly roar and the two of them began communicating with a combination of sounds and gestures.

The students stared in confusion as they watched the weird friendship between them. Mr. Black brushed off his clothes and approached the students with a wide smile on his face. "Everyone, let me introduce you to my old friend,

Chico," he said, gesturing towards the gorilla who was standing nearby.

"Chico and I go way back. We met here in these woods when I was first exploring the Sanctuary. It's been quite a few years now, and we've been having this ongoing game of trying to surprise and win a fight over each other," Mr. Black explained with a chuckle.

The students looked at each other in amazement. They had never heard of someone being friends with a gorilla before. Aria asked, "How did you two even become friends in the first place?"

"Well, it started out as a challenge," Mr. Black said, his eyes twinkling. "I was trying to find my way through these woods, and Chico came out of nowhere, trying to scare me. But instead of run away, I stood my ground, and we ended up having a little wrestling match. And from there, we just hit it off."

"Wow, that's amazing," Ethan said, impressed. "Do you talk to each other?"

"Not in the traditional sense, no," Mr. Black replied. "But we have our own way of communicating. Sounds, gestures, body language, you know. We understand each other quite well."

Chico made a few grunts and hand gestures, and Mr. Black laughed. "See what I mean?" he said to the students. They all smiled, still in disbelief at what they were witnessing.

As the students gathered around Chico, Mr. Black called the students, "Alright everyone, we must get going." The students all said goodbye to Chico, who waved back with a huge smile on his face.

As they walked, the students chattered excitedly about the fight they had just witnessed. "Did you see the way Mr. Black held his own against Chico?" said Aria, "I had no idea he was that strong."

"I know right!" replied Isabella, "I was so scared for him at first, but then he just took control. It was amazing!"

Ethan chimed in, "I can't believe he's been friends with a gorilla for all these years. That's just wild!"

Michael added, "Yeah, I thought gorillas were supposed to be mean and dangerous, but Chico was actually really nice. I'm glad Mr. Black made a friend like that."

As they talked, the students all seemed to be in agreement that Mr. Black was one of the coolest people they had ever met, and they couldn't wait to see what other adventures awaited them on their trip to Mount Mystic.

Finally, after an difficult hike up the mountain, the group of students reached the peak of Mount Mystic. The view from the top was breathtaking. From the peak, they could see the lush green forests, the vast blue sky, and the distant camp where they had set up their tents. Marcus, who had been complaining about the hike the whole way, finally fell silent. He stood there with his mouth agape, taking in the beauty of the scene before him.

"Wow," Emma whispered, "look at the view. I can even see the Falls of the Moon from here."

"And the camp," Isabella added, "it's so small from up here."

Marcus let out a sigh, "I'm just glad we made it to the top. I wasn't sure my legs were going to make it."

Mr. Black chuckled, "It's worth it though, isn't it? The view is stunning."

Ethan was still in awe of the view. He had never seen anything like it before. "It's amazing," he said. "I'm glad we came here."

As the students sat at the peak of Mount Mystic, breathing heavily from the hike, Mr. Black stood in front of them, looking out at the stunning scenery. He began to speak, his voice deep and full of wisdom.

"Do you all know the story of Mount Mystic?" he asked, looking around at the eager faces of the students. "This mountain has been a sacred place for generations. It is said that long ago, the powerful sorcerers of the land gathered here to perform a spell of great importance."

Mr. Black continued, "The spell was meant to protect the land from evil forces and keep peace and prosperity for all. But, as the sorcerers were casting their spell, a powerful being of darkness appeared and interrupted their ritual. A fierce battle erupted, with the sorcerers using their magic to fight against the dark being."

"In the end, the sorcerers emerged victorious, but at a great cost. They had used all of their magic and were left exhausted and vulnerable. The dark being was banished, but it is said that its evil influence still lingers, waiting for the right moment to return."

As Mr. Black finished his tale, a silence fell over the group. The students looked around at the beautiful, yet mysterious landscape.

Marcus spoke up, breaking the silence. "That's a pretty scary story, Mr. Black," he said, shivering.

"But it just goes to show the power of good and the importance of standing up against evil," replied Mr. Black, his voice steady.

As the group sat in silence, taking in the majestic view, filled with awe and wonder at the story of Mount Mystic and the bravery of the sorcerers.

After a while, Mr. Black reminded the students that they needed to start heading back to camp. The students groaned, but they knew it was time to start their descent. They started the hike back down to the camp, making their way through the forest and over the rocky terrain.

When they arrived at the camp, the students were starving and ready for lunch. They quickly set up their camp chairs and dug into their packed lunches, chatting and laughing as they ate. The students were all in high spirits, feeling proud of themselves for making the hike up Mount Mystic.

After eating their fill, the students sprang into action, busying themselves with the task of packing up camp. They meticulously checked and rechecked their belongings, making sure not a single item was left behind. Tents were rolled up, sleeping bags packed away, and any other gear was securely stowed. Meanwhile, Mr. Black gathered the students for a group stretching session, ensuring that everyone was physically prepared for the journey back to the Sanctuary.

With muscles loosened and gear stowed, the group set out on the trail, ready for the hike ahead.

As the students hiked back to the Sanctuary, they were tired but still in good spirits. They chatted and laughed, making jokes and telling stories. Aria pointed out different wildlife they saw along the way, like a group of squirrels playing in the trees.

Finally, the students arrived back at the Sanctuary, exhausted but exhilarated from their journey. They all said their goodbyes to Mr. Black and headed to their dorms, already looking forward to their next adventure in the Sanctuary.

CHAPTER 17

A TASTE OF THE PAST

Ethan, Marcus, and Emma sat at a table in the school cafeteria, eating their breakfast as they talked about the approaching winter. Marcus was excited about the shorter days, as it meant more time for him to be awake and active. "I can't wait for winter," he said with a grin. "Less naps during the day for me."

Emma, on the other hand, had a different perspective. As a bear Animalian, she had an urge to hibernate during the colder months. "I don't know, I feel like I'm going to be so tired all the time," she said, stifling a yawn. "I might just sleep through the whole weekend."

Ethan laughed, "Well, at least you won't have to worry about being late for class."

The three friends laughed and continued to chat as they finished their breakfast.

As Marcus sat at the table in the school cafeteria, his eyes caught sight of Sarah across the room. She was walking by, her head held high and a determined look on her face. Marcus couldn't help but watch her intently, his gaze following her every move.

Ethan, who was sitting next to him, noticed his friend's behavior and raised an eyebrow. "Dude, what are you staring at?"

Marcus quickly snapped out of his trance, turning to face Ethan with a sheepish grin. "Oh, nothing. Just keeping an eye out for anything suspicious. You know, since she might be related to the poisonings and all."

Ethan rolled his eyes, but didn't push the issue further. Just then, Sarah caught sight of the three friends and waved at them. Marcus, caught off guard, let out an awkward wave and made a strange face.

"Smooth, Marcus," Ethan teased, chuckling.

"Shut up," Marcus grumbled, his cheeks turning red with embarrassment.

"Hey guys," Alex said as he walked up to them. "Have you heard about the poisonings? Some students and their parents are really worried about the safety of the school after what happened to Ms. Park. Some of them are even thinking about withdrawing for the year."

Ethan nodded, "Yeah, it's pretty crazy. We were just talking about it before you came over."

Emma chimed in, "I know, it's so scary. I can't believe someone would do something like that to Ms. Park. I hope they catch the person responsible soon."

Alex nodded, "Me too. Rumors has it that might be one of the students here. But I can't imagine anyone from our school doing something like that."

Ethan shrugged, "I don't know. People can surprise you. But hopefully, the school will figure out what's going on and keep us all safe."

"Yeah," Alex said, his voice quiet. "I just hope they catch the person before anyone else gets hurt."

The three friends sat in silence for a moment, lost in their own thoughts about the recent events. The school's safety was a serious concern for everyone, and they all hoped that the person responsible would be caught soon.

The trio, Ethan, Emma and Marcus, walked into the Animalian History classroom. The room was large and dimly lit, with rows of desks and chairs facing a large whiteboard at the front of the room. George Smith, the aged but wise teacher, was already seated at his desk, shuffling through some papers. As the students took their seats, George looked up and greeted them with a smile.

"Good morning, class," he said, in his strong and clear voice. "Today, we will be discussing conflicts that have occurred throughout Animalian history. It is important for us to understand the past, so that we can learn from it and avoid making the same mistakes in the future."

Marcus, Ethan, and Emma listened intently as George began to speak about the various conflicts that have occurred throughout Animalian history. He spoke of the Great War between the different Animalian tribes, and the alliance that was formed between the bears, wolves, and lions to defeat the invading army of snakes. He spoke of the rise of the tyrannical leader, who sought to conquer and enslave all other Animalian tribes. He told about the brave heroes who stood against him and the sacrifices they made to bring about peace and freedom.

As George spoke, the students listened in awe, captivated by the stories of bravery, sacrifice, and the struggles for freedom. They were amazed by the depth of knowledge and understanding that George possessed, and the way he was able to make even the most complicated historical events easy to understand.

Ethan raised his hand and asked George about a specific battle and how it ended, George smiled and replied "That's a great question Ethan, the battle ended with a great sacrifice from a young lion Animalian who managed to sneak behind enemy lines and took out the leader, it was a turning point in the war and it allowed the alliance to push forward and win the war."

Ethan raised his hand again and asked, "Mr. Smith, I know this is slightly off topic, but I've always been curious. Who were the most powerful Animalians in history?" George smiled and leaned back in his chair, his eyes becoming distant as he began to recall the past.

"Ah, a question of great interest to many young Animalians. The answer, my dear Ethan, is a complex one. The concept of 'power' can be interpreted in many ways, and there are many examples of Animalians throughout history who have been powerful in different ways. However, if we're talking about raw physical power, then there are a few individuals who stand out above the rest."

George began to pace back and forth in front of the class, his voice growing more animated as he spoke. "One of the most powerful Animalians in history was a bear Animalian named Koda. He was said to be nearly invulnerable, able to withstand even the strongest of attacks. His strength and endurance were legendary, and he was said to have been able to lift entire trees with ease. He lived during the Great War and was a fierce warrior who fought bravely for his people."

"Another powerful Animalian was a lion named Muasa. He had a presence that commanded respect and fear, and his roar could shake the earth. He was a great leader, and his wisdom and courage were respected by many. He was also a gifted strategist, and his tactics were said to have been instrumental in many of the battles he fought in."

"And finally, one of the most renowned was an electric eel Animalian who could cause thunderstorms with a mere thought. Also, more recently, we had an ex-student here at the Sanctuary who possessed the power of a chameleon, he developed his camouflage ability so much he was able to shape shift and even regrow lost limbs."

George paused, his gaze sweeping over the class. "These are just a few examples, my dear students. There are many more powerful Animalians throughout history, each with their own unique abilities and strengths. It is important to remember that power comes in many forms, and that true strength is not measured by physical prowess alone, but also by wisdom, courage, and integrity."

Emma raised her hand next. "Sir, if you don't mind me asking, have there ever been any threats to the Sanctuary before?"

George's eyes took on a faraway look, as if he were lost in a distant memory. "Yes, my dear. There have been many threats to the Sanctuary throughout its history. Some were from outside forces, trying to exploit the power of the Animalians for their own gain. Others were from within, from those who wanted to use their abilities for personal gain or to cause harm. Some were more serious than others, but all were dangerous in their own way."

Ethan's curiosity was piqued. "Can you give us some examples, sir?"

"Of course," George replied. "One of the most notable threat was the Great War of the Animalians. It was a brutal and bloody conflict that lasted for over a decade. Many lives were lost, and the Sanctuary was nearly destroyed. But with the help of powerful Animalians like the bear and the lion, we were able to repel the enemy and restore peace."

"But perhaps the most dangerous threat we face was against something so tiny you can't even see it." George cleared his throat and leaned back in his chair, his eyes taking on a distant look as he began to speak. "There was a time, many years ago, when the Sanctuary faced a threat that we never could have imagined. It was an outbreak of a contagious disease that spread rapidly among the Animalians living here. It was a dark and trying time for all of us."

He continued, "the first signs of the disease appeared suddenly and without warning. One day, a student came to class feeling unwell and with a high fever. We thought it was just a simple cold or flu, but within hours, other students began to show similar symptoms. Soon, the entire campus was in a state of panic as the disease spread rapidly among our community."

The teacher's voice tumbled a bit, "the Sanctuary's staff and faculty worked tirelessly to contain the outbreak, but it was a losing battle. The disease was highly contagious and seemed to be resistant to all of our treatments. It was unlike anything we had ever seen before. Many of the students and staff fell ill, and we were forced to isolate those who were infected to prevent further spread of the disease. It was a difficult and heart-wrenching decision, as we watched our friends and loved ones suffer. But in the face of such adversity, we came together as a community. The healthy students and staff worked together to care for the sick, and we did everything in our power to keep the Sanctuary running. We set up quarantine areas and implemented strict hygiene protocols to prevent further spread of the disease. Despite our efforts, the death toll was high. Many of our students and staff lost their lives to the disease. It was a tragic and difficult time for all of us, and it was a reminder that even in a place like the Sanctuary, where we were supposed to be safe and protected, danger could still find us."

George's voice was heavy with emotion as he finished his story, "but even in the darkest of times, there is always hope. Eventually, the disease began to dissipate and the number of new cases began to decline. We were able to start rebuilding our community and moving forward, stronger and more united than ever before."

There was a moment of silence in the classroom as his students absorbed the gravity of what he had shared. Emma, Marcus, and Ethan sat in silence, their faces etched with sadness and empathy. They knew that the Sanctuary was not immune to the dangers of the world, but they also knew that they were strong enough to overcome any obstacle as long as they stood together.

CHAPTER 18

A GLIDING INVESTIGATION

Ethan woke up early on Saturday morning, feeling refreshed and energized. He decided to take advantage of the beautiful weather and go for a run in the Sanctuary's fields. The sun was shining, and a gentle breeze blew through the trees, rustling the leaves. Ethan felt alive and free, his heart pounding in his chest.

As he ran, Ethan's thoughts turned to his Animalian powers. He was proud of his abilities, but he knew that he still had much to learn and much to improve upon. He focused on pushing himself to run faster and further, feeling the burn in his muscles and the sweat on his skin.

Ethan noticed a movement out of the corner of his eye. He turned his head to see Talon, the majestic and powerful falcon, gliding effortlessly through the air. Talon was a friend of Ethan, and they had spent many hours together talking and exploring the Sanctuary.

Ethan was filled with awe and inspiration as he watched Talon gracefully glide through the air. He felt a sudden urge to join the falcon and feel the wind beneath his wings. He started to give small jumps and soon enough he felt like he was gliding. He kept pushing himself, focusing on the sensation of lifting off the ground and soaring through the air.

Ethan was feeling light and realized he was indeed gliding. He was able to glide several yards with a single leap. That was a huge improvement on his abilities and he felt exhilaration rush through him.

Ethan was feeling the burn in his muscles as he made his way back to his dormitory. The cold fall air had done little to cool him down, and he was sweating profusely despite the chill in the air. As he walked through the empty halls, he heard two familiar voices arguing around the corner. He couldn't quite make out what they were saying, but he recognized the voices as belonging to Mr. Black and Braveheart.

Curious, Ethan quickened his pace, trying to get closer to the source of the argument. As he approached the corner, he heard Mr. Black and Braveheart walking in his direction, their voices raised in heated discussion.

"This can't go on," Mr. Black was saying, his voice tight with frustration.

"You need to decide if you trust me or not," Braveheart shot back, his voice equally intense.

Ethan stand there, trying to listen in on their conversation. Mr. Black responded with "Of course I trust you, but maybe you are wrong."

But as soon as they turned the corner and Ethan was in their view, they stopped talking and acknowledged him with a nod. They continued talking in a lower, indistinguishable voice and walked away from Ethan.

Ethan was left standing there, confused and slightly bewildered. He had no idea what they were talking about, but he could sense the tension between them. He wondered what could be causing such a strong disagreement between the two respected members of the Sanctuary staff.

Ethan walked into his dorm room after a shower, still feeling the rush of adrenaline from his successful glide. He found Emma and Marcus sitting on his bed, deep in conversation. "Hey, what's up?" he asked, as he grabbed a towel to dry off his damp hair.

"We were just talking about what you heard," Emma said, her brow furrowed in concern. "Do you think Mr. Black shared the piece of paper with 'Leo' on it with Braveheart?"

Ethan thought for a moment before responding. "I'm not sure, but it definitely looks like Mr. Black is torn between believing Braveheart or not," he said, as he sat down on his own bed. "I mean, I overheard Braveheart saying that Mr. Black would have to make a decision about trusting him or not."

"That's what we thought too," Marcus chimed in. "But why would Mr. Black be questioning Braveheart's trustworthiness? He's always seemed so loyal to the Sanctuary, and Mr. Black said to us he trusted Braveheart completely."

"I don't know," Ethan admitted. "But it seems like there's something going on that we don't know about."

Marcus nodded. "If this counts as evidence, we have more clues pointing to Braveheart than anyone else," he said, crossing his arms.

Emma had a sudden thought. "But what if Mr. Black is also behind it, helping Braveheart?" she asked, her eyes widening.

Ethan shook his head. "I don't believe that. I trust Mr. Black. Plus, why would he help poison Ms. Park, who's a great friend of his?" he said, looking at Emma and Marcus with a determined expression.

The three of them sat in silence for a moment, pondering the possibility. Emma bit her lip and looked at Ethan. "You're right, I don't think he would do that either. We just have to keep an eye on the situation and see what happens," she said, nodding.

"You know who would really be able to help us with all this puzzling information?" Marcus said, his voice tinged with excitement. "Sarah! She is super smart and can definitely look at all this logically."

Emma looked at Marcus skeptically and said, "I'm not sure if I trust her. Remember, she being a suspect and all?"

"Trust me in this one, okay?" Marcus replied.

Emma hesitated for a moment before nodding. "Okay, let's do it. But, we have to be careful. We don't know who to trust or what's going on."

Ethan and Marcus nodded in agreement, and the trio set off to find Sarah and get to the bottom of this mystery once and for all.

Marcus took them to the most likely place Sarah could be: the library, a grand, imposing building with tall, arched windows and a looming stone façade. As they walked through the doors, the smell of old books and the hushed whispers of students filled their nostrils and ears. The library was a maze of shelves, stacked high with books of all shapes and sizes. The shelves were made of dark wood and the books had a musty smell. The library was well lit, with quite a few small lamps casting light on the stacks of books. The three of them walked through the maze of shelves, searching for Sarah.

Ethan spotted her first, sitting at a table surrounded by books and papers, her bright blonde hair a beacon of light. Marcus spotted her too, even though he didn't have a falcon eye. They made their way over to her, Marcus sheepishly greeting her.

"Hey Sarah, can we talk to you for a bit?" Marcus asked.

Sarah looked up from her book, her bright green eyes curious. "Sure," she said, closing the book and marking her place with a piece of paper.

"Shhh!" Another student shushed them, so Sarah suggested they move to a group study area where they could talk.

They walked to another area where they found an empty table, and other students deep in their books. As they sat down Emma started the conversation "We need to talk to you about something important, do you know what we are talking about?"

Sarah looked up at them, her expression curious. "Our only conversation was about the poisoning incident, so I suspect that's the topic," she said.

Ethan, Emma, and Marcus exchanged a glance, confirming that she was indeed correct. "Yes, that's what we want to talk to you about," Emma said.

"Have you decided to trust me?" Sarah asked, her green eyes sharp and alert.

Marcus gave her a strange smile. "I never distrusted you, Sarah," he said.

Sarah nodded, understanding. "Okay... Alright, let's talk," she said, with a slight smile. Despite the constant flow of students entering and exiting the room, the trio remained focused and undistracted by the commotion around them.

"We have some clues about what's been happening, but we can't seem to piece them together," Marcus said. She nodded for him to continue. "Alright, so let me start from the beginning. When Elmer was poisoned, Ethan noticed a student rushing out of the classroom, limping," Marcus began, his eyes focused on Sarah as she listened intently. "We later found out that the student was Jack, who is a snake Animalian. But when we confronted him, he denied even being in that class. To be fair, we haven't seen him in that class since, and the times we seen him the limping was gone," Marcus finished, a hint of frustration in his voice.

Sarah furrowed her brow in thought. "Hmm, that's strange. But it doesn't mean he's innocent. Maybe he's just trying to deceive you. Do you have any other clues?"

As Marcus continued to speak, he revealed the next piece of evidence in their investigation. "The next clue involves you," he said, looking directly at Sarah. "On the day of the coyotes poisoning, Doug said he smelled a scent that he only smelled once before, during Braveheart's welcoming speech, coming from you..."

Sarah interrupted, a look of confusion and concern etched on her face. "But I wasn't there," she protested. "Well, from your perspective I could be lying. Did he ever smell that scent again? In me or elsewhere?"

Ethan spoke up, his voice calm and steady. "As far as we know, he hasn't," he said.

Sarah nodded, her mind clearly racing as she processed the information. "I understand why you might suspect me," she said. "But after the ceremony, I've been in contact with Doug several times. If it was really me, he would have probably smelled it again by now."

Marcus and Ethan exchanged a glance, both clearly unsure of how to respond. Sarah's argument made sense, but the evidence against her was still there. They needed more information before they could come to any conclusions.

Ethan continued, "Then there is what happened to Ms. Park. As I walked past her office, the door was slightly open and I felt something was off. So, I went to check it out. When I opened the door, I saw Ms. Park sitting on a chair slumped over her desk, unconscious. And near her, there was a piece of paper with 'Leo' written on it. Seconds later, Braveheart and another teacher came in the room, so I hid the piece of paper."

Sarah responded with a sharp nod, "And now you suspect that Leo Braveheart did it."

Emma replied positively, "Yes, it is a strong piece of evidence."

Sarah, said thoughtfully, "This is a strong evidence, but it could also mean other things. Maybe the note was incomplete, maybe she wanted to send a message to Braveheart, or maybe it's just a misdirection. Maybe it wasn't even Ms. Park who wrote it."

Ethan replied with a confident nod, "It seems like Ms. Park's handwriting, and trust me, I can notice very subtle differences. The note was written in the same handwriting as Ms. Park's texts that I've seen."

Sarah leaned forward in her chair, her eyes fixed on Ethan as she asked, "And have you shown this piece of paper to anyone else?"

Ethan hesitated for a moment before responding, "We did. We showed it to Mr. Black, but he was convinced that Braveheart had nothing to do with it."

Sarah's eyebrows furrowed in confusion. "Really? What made him so certain?"

Ethan shrugged. "I don't know. They've know each other for a long time, I guess. But later, I overheard a conversation between them. They seemed to be disagreeing about something, and Braveheart was insisting that Mr. Black needed to decide if he trusted him or not."

Sarah nodded slowly, her thoughts rushing as she tried to make sense of the information. "And what did Mr. Black say?"

"He said that he trusted Braveheart, but that maybe he was wrong," Ethan replied.

Sarah leaned back in her chair, deep in thought. "This is all very incriminating," she said after a moment. "But it could also mean nothing at all," she shrug with a subtle smile.

Marcus spoke up. "That's all we've got," he said, looking around at his friends. "What do you think, Sarah?"

Sarah was contemplative for a moment, trying to piece together the clues and understand the situation. "Well, it's very inconclusive for sure," she began. "You have a lead that points to Jack, another that points to me, and a stronger one to Braveheart. The poisoning looking like reptile venom and Jack being a snake Animalian makes a good narrative, but me and Jack, we both stated that we weren't where we were allegedly supposed to be. So, if you choose to believe us, then there are a few possibilities to explain that."

Ethan, Marcus and Emma listened intently as Sarah continued. "One is that we may have been tinkered with to be manipulated and forgot what happened. I've read about these insects that can basically infiltrate another insects brains and mind control them, although I never heard about an Animalian with that power, but you never know. Another explanation is that it wasn't us, there are a few shapeshifters documented in Animalian history and this could be one of them."

Sarah shifted her focus to the lead involving Braveheart. "As for the leads to Braveheart, they are strong but still inconclusive. The fact Mr. Black trusts him makes it problematic, either Mr. Black is being deceived or he is involved. Either way, you need more information."

The trio sat there taking in all that information. They were impressed by Sarah's intelligence and logic reasoning. Marcus let out a impressed "wow."

Sarah smiled, "I may not be a detective, but I do have a knack for putting pieces together."

"Thanks, Sarah," Ethan said as he smiled at her. "We really appreciate your help."

"Yeah, you're a lifesaver," Emma added.

Sarah looked up at them and smiled. "No problem, I'm happy to help."

As they were about to leave, Marcus turned to her and cleared his throat. "Umm, Sarah, I was wondering if maybe we could, umm, talk about all of this some more? Just, you know, to discuss the events and all," he added, trying to sound casual but failing miserably.

Sarah raised an eyebrow, a small smile playing on her lips. "Sure, Marcus. I'd be happy to discuss it with you."

Marcus felt his face turn red as he stuttered a quick "Great, umm, I'll be in touch." He turned and quickly followed Ethan and Emma out of the room, leaving Sarah sitting in her chair, still smiling to herself. As they walked down the hallway, Ethan turned to Marcus and playfully punched him in the arm.

"Dude, you totally have a crush on her," he laughed.

Marcus let out a nervous chuckle. "Shh, man. Don't say that so loud."

Emma shook her head, smiling. "You're so obvious, Marcus. But I have to say, I don't blame you. Sarah is pretty amazing."

As they made their way out of the building, Marcus felt excitement and anticipation for their next meeting with Sarah. He knew he needed to focus on the investigation, but he couldn't help but let his mind wander to the possibility of something more with the smart and intriguing Sarah.

CHAPTER 19

FERAL FLAG

Ethan groggily woke up to the sound of knocking on his door. He rubbed his eyes and looked around the dimly lit room, trying to remember where he was. Then he heard the voices of Isabella and Emma, and it all came back to him.

"Hey, Ethan, are you ready for the Feral Flag game? We've been waiting for you," Isabella said, her voice full of excitement.

Ethan looked at his watch and saw that it was almost time for the game. He quickly got out of bed and started getting dressed. "Yeah, I'm coming. Just give me a few minutes."

As he finished putting on his shoes, he saw Marcus stirring in his bed. "Hey man, are you coming to the game with us?" Ethan asked.

Marcus groaned and rolled over. "Nah, I don't feel like it. You guys go ahead without me."

Ethan shrugged and grabbed his backpack, ready to head out. "Suit yourself, man. See you later."

Isabella and Emma were waiting outside, and they started walking towards the field where the Feral Flag game was going to take place. As they walked, they chatted about their Animalian abilities and what strategy they were going to use to win the game.

Ethan felt a little left out, having never played Feral Flag before. "So how exactly does this game work?" he asked, feeling a little lost.

Isabella grinned, "It's basically like capture the flag, but with Animalian abilities!" she exclaimed, gesturing animatedly with her hands. "The objective is to capture the other team's flag and bring it back to your own field without getting tackled by the other team. The only rule is that if you have a flying ability, you can't fly above ground level carrying the flag."

Emma nodded in agreement, "And if you do get tackled, you have to go back to your own field before trying again. It can get pretty intense."

Isabella giggled, "But don't worry, nobody's died playing Feral Flag. At least, not in this decade," she joked, winking at Ethan.

Ethan felt a rush of excitement as he listened to Emma and Isabella explain the rules of the game. The way they described it made it sound like a thrilling adventure. As they walked towards the field, Ethan could feel his heart pounding with anticipation.

"Wow, this game sounds awesome," Ethan said, grinning from ear to ear.

"It is! Just wait until you see it in action," Isabella replied.

As they approached the field, Ethan took a deep breath, ready to give it his all. The sun was shining bright and the grass was a vibrant green. He looked around and saw other students gathering, chatting excitedly as they prepared for the game. He recognized a few faces from his grade, including Alex and the Stone brothers, but there were also some people from other grades he had never met before.

The game field was a vast expanse of land, surrounded by dense trees and foliage. The playing area was divided into two sections by a line of rocks, arranged in a row but not high enough to block people from jumping over it. The ground was a mix of lush green grass and patches of dirt, providing a challenging terrain for the players.

The playing area was filled with multiple kinds of obstacles and features. There were tall trees with branches so big people could walk over them, boulders scattered throughout the field, and a lake in the center that provided a formidable barrier for anyone trying to cross it. At one end of the field, there was a tunnel over a hill, providing a thrilling and strategic route for players to take.

The flags were set up at the end of each section, designed with the Sanctuary emblem. One flag was blue, and the other was golden, representing the two opposing teams. The flags were hoisted on tall poles, visible from all corners of the field.

The Stone brothers stood in a tight group, smirking as they looked in Ethan's direction. Ethan felt a twinge of apprehension, knowing how the Stone Brothers could be.

"Hey, Ethan," Jake said, drawing out each word. "Ready to get crushed in the game today?"

Tyler and Zack chuckled, clearly relishing in the teasing. Ethan tried to ignore them, but their words still stung.

"I don't think you can keep up with us," Tyler added, his voice dripping with contempt.

Ethan squared his shoulders and tried to keep his voice even. "We'll see about that. I'm not afraid of a little competition."

Isabella totally ignored the Stone brothers and led Ethan over to a group of Animalians who were gathered together, chatting and laughing amongst themselves. "Ethan, I want you to meet Jafari," she said, gesturing towards the young African man with the cheetah spirit. "He's one of the fastest runners in the Sanctuary."

Jafari gave Ethan a friendly nod and a smile. "Nice to meet you, man. Isabella's told me all about you. You're the new guy, right? Ready to show us what you've got on the field?" he asked, a playful glint in his eye.

Next, Isabella introduced Ethan to Willow, a young teenager with fair skin and a spirit of a frog. "Willow is an exceptional jumper," she explained. "She can also use her long, sticky tongue to grab onto things and pull herself up."

Willow beamed at Ethan, hopping up and down on the balls of her feet. "Hi there! It's so great to meet you. I can't wait to see what you can do on the field," she said, her green eyes sparkling with excitement.

As Isabella led Ethan further into the group, they came upon Remy, a tall and muscular young man with tan skin and short black hair. "Remy is incredibly strong and durable," Isabella explained, "and he has the ability to charge forward with great force, much like a rhinoceros. I would recommend to not stand in his way."

Remy gave Ethan a firm handshake, his grayish eyes meeting his with a steady gaze. "Pleasure to meet you," he said in a deep, rumbling voice.

Isabella led Ethan over to another tall, muscular young man who was standing with his arms crossed, surveying the field with a serious expression. "Ethan, this is Finn," she said, gesturing towards the young man. "He's got the spirit of a shark, so watch out." Finn turned to face them, his piercing gaze assessing Ethan with a sharp intensity. He had a chiseled jawline and a bald head that glistened in the sun, and his powerful build exuded an air of quiet confidence. As he spoke, his voice was low and measured, with a hint of a growl that sent shivers down Ethan's spine. "Good to meet you, Ethan," Finn said, extending a hand.

Finally, Isabella introduced Ethan to Aurora, a young woman with the spirit of a hummingbird. "Aurora is very agile, and she can fly and dance in the air," Isabella said with a smile.

Aurora gave Ethan a graceful bow, her bright purple hair shimmering in the sunlight. "It's wonderful to meet you, Ethan. I can't wait to see you soar," she said, her voice light and airy.

As the group chatted and laughed together, Ethan felt a strong sense of belonging. The Animalians were all so unique and different, yet they all shared a common bond. However, he felt a wave of self-doubt wash over him as he took in the impressive abilities of his new acquaintances. Compared to their animal-like abilities, his own falcon talent seemed insignificant. Would he be able to keep up with the other players? Would he be able to make a meaningful contribution to the team? These thoughts weighed heavily on Ethan's mind, but he tried his best to keep them hidden beneath a mask of confidence.

Ethan and the others formed a circle as they prepared to divide into teams. Jafari announced they should split into two teams of six, and after some deliberation, they eventually settled on the Stone brothers, Remy, Finn, and Aurora on one team, and Ethan, Emma, Isabella, Jafari, Alex, and Willow on the other. "All right," Remy said, clapping his hands together.

The two teams split up and began strategizing. As the team gathered around their flag, Jafari took the lead and began to lay out the general strategy for the game. "Alright, Emma and Alex, you two will be our line of defense. Your strength is critical for keeping the enemy away from our flag. Ethan, your advantage is your aerial mobility. Keep an eye on Aurora and see if you can catch her in the air. Willow, your job is to keep an eye on Finn. If he goes in the water, you're the only one who can catch him. Isabella and I will try to get the flag, but we need to be careful with Remy. Once he charges forward, it's nearly impossible to tackle him."

Emma and Alex nodded in agreement, ready to defend their territory. Ethan felt relieved knowing that his unique ability would be useful for their team, and he was determined to make the most of it. Willow, who had been quiet until now, gave a nod to show that she understood her role in the game. Isabella and Jafari shared a look of determination, ready to face the challenge ahead.

"Remember, our goal is to protect our flag while trying to capture the enemy's," Jafari said. "If we can hold them off long enough, we can wear them down and make our move. But we need to be smart about it. Any questions?"

The team shook their heads, and Jafari grinned. "Good. Let's get out there and show them what we're made of." As the group made their way to their starting positions, Ethan felt a surge of excitement. He was ready to put his abilities to the test and make his team proud.

Everyone got in position, the energy palpable in the air as they checked their surroundings for any signs of the other team. Once they were sure they were ready, the Stone brothers gave a nod to their team. Jafari did the same to Ethan's team.

"Alright, everyone! Get ready, we'll count down from 5!" Remy shouted.

"5, 4, 3, 2, 1!" Remy counted down with Jafari.

As soon as they said "1," both teams sprinted towards the center of the field.

Jafari dashed forward towards the enemy's field. Isabella, on the other hand, was more cautious, using her jaguar-like abilities to blend into the shadows and move unnoticed.

Willow leaped high into the air and went towards the lake in the center.

The Stone brothers stayed back in defense, with their coyote-like agility and quick reflexes making them a tough team to get past. Meanwhile, Remy, Finn, and Aurora charged forward on the offensive, their animal-like powers allowing them to move with incredible speed and agility.

Jafari managed to make it to the enemy side with his incredible speed, his cheetah-like quadrupedal movements making him hard to catch. Remy, who had been charging forward to take out anyone who crossed his path, was completely caught off guard by Jafari's sudden appearance. Jafari easily dodged Remy's attack, moving like a blur across the field.

Ethan kept his eyes on the sky, watching as Aurora flitted back and forth, always staying just out of reach. Even though he couldn't fly, he was determined to keep up with her. He sprinted across the field, following her movements from the ground. As he ran, he felt the wind rushing past him, his senses heightened by the adrenaline pumping through his veins.

Isabella, on the other hand, had taken to the trees. She moved from branch to branch with the grace of a jaguar, her sharp senses alert for any sign of danger. From her perch high above the field, she could see everything that was happening, her eyes scanning the area for any sign of the enemy team. Her plan was to go undetected through the enemy field and reach the flag unnoticed.

Jafari got closer and closer to the flag, his cheetah abilities allowing him to outrun anyone in his path. As he reached the halfway point, he could see the flag fluttering in the breeze. Suddenly, he saw two figures standing in front of the flag, the Stone brothers.

Tyler and Zack smirked as they saw Jafari approaching, but Jafari was too quick for them. He dodged Tyler with a quick juke and then zigzagged to avoid Zack. As he made his way past the Stone brothers, he could see the flag in his sights.

As Jafari close in the flag, he heard a loud splash in the lake. He turned his head to see Finn swimming at lightning-fast speeds. Jafari knew he had to hurry before Finn made his way to the flag.

Jafari leaped forward, but just as he was about to grab the flag, he felt a sudden impact from the side. He looked up and saw Jake Stone tackling him to the ground.

"Nice try, cheetah boy," Jake sneered. "But we're not gonna make it easy for you to win this game."

Jafari quickly got up, brushing off the dirt from his clothes. "The game isn't over yet," Jafari said, determination in his voice.

Finn emerged from the water on the other side of the lake, he seemed energized and refreshed after being in the water. As he stepped onto the ground, he suddenly felt something wrap around his ankle. Startled, he looked down to see Willow's long frog tongue coiled around his leg. With a sudden yank, she pulled him off balance and he stumbled to the ground.

"What the... hey, let me go!" Finn sputtered as he struggled to free himself from Willow's grip. But the young frog Animalian was too quick for him. In a flash, she leaped onto his chest and tagged him with her hand, grinning in triumph.

"Gotcha!" she exclaimed, pumping her fist in the air. "You're out!"

Finn groaned, feeling a mixture of frustration and admiration for Willow's quick reflexes. "Nice one, Willow," he said, giving her a rueful smile. "I guess I should have seen that coming."

As Remy charged forward with great force, his rhinoceros abilities giving him an edge, Emma braced herself to try and stop him. But even with her bear strength, she couldn't hold back the charging beast. Alex, the small and skinny boy with the power of an ant, saw Emma struggling and knew he had to act fast. With a quick leap, he landed on Remy's back, holding on tightly for dear life.

Remy was momentarily surprised by the sudden weight on his back, but his determination to reach the flag kept him moving forward. However, as he reached the flag and grabbed it with one hand, he began to slow down to turn around and head back towards his own field. It was at this moment that Alex saw his opportunity. With a quick burst of strength, he lifted Remy off the ground and threw him to the side, causing Remy to crash to the ground with a loud thud.

Aurora had been scanning the field from the sky, looking for the perfect opportunity to swoop down and snatch the flag. As she saw Remy being tackled to the ground, she knew that this was her chance. With lightning-fast reflexes, she dived towards the flag and scooped it up, taking off in a blur of motion. Emma and Alex tried to catch her, but she was too quick for them.

As Aurora flew back at near ground level towards her own field, Ethan watched while running, calculating the perfect angle to intercept her. He spotted a large boulder and made a beeline for it, using it to launch himself into the air. Gliding down towards Aurora, he landed on her back, surprising her with his sudden appearance. They both tumbled onto the ground in a heap, surrounded by a bed of soft plants that cushion the fall.

"Nice try," Ethan said, grinning at Aurora as he got to his feet, flag in hand.

Aurora laughed and brushed herself off. "You caught me off guard," she said, admiring Ethan's speed and agility.

As the tagged people went back to their sides, Isabella felt a thrill of excitement as she moved with stealth and agility through the trees, making her way towards the enemy flag. She had always been good at moving quietly, and her jaguar spirit made her even more adept at it. As she made her way through the tunnel, she had a surge of adrenaline as she saw the flag within her reach.

She reached out and grabbed the flag, but as she turned around, she saw the Stone brothers looking right at her. "Hey, she's got our flag!" Jake yelled, and the three of them started sprinting towards her.

Isabella started to run, but the Stone brothers were hot on her trail. She zigzagged through the trees, hoping to lose them, but they were too fast and too coordinated. As she tried to zigzag and jump from branch to branch, Finn spotted her from afar and realized what was happening. He quickly joined forces with the Stone brothers. They managed to corner her, but Isabella wasn't about to go down without a fight.

Ethan, who had been on the other side of the field, saw what was happening and quickly made his way towards the commotion.

"Looks like you guys finally found me," Isabella said with a smirk. "But I won't give up this easily." She leapt down from the trees and landed in a crouch, ready to fight. The Stone brothers and Finn closed in, circling her like predators closing in on their prey.

As Isabella saw Jake coming for her, she took a deep breath and braced herself for the tackle. But then, out of nowhere, Ethan swooped in and grabbed the flag from her, quickly jumping high and away from the defenders of the flag. Isabella was momentarily stunned but quickly regained her composure and turned to see Ethan leaping and dodging around the enemy players, his agility and speed on full display. She was amazed at the way he moved, almost like a bird in flight.

As Ethan approached his team's field, he felt his heart pounding in his chest. He was so close to victory, but he also knew that the game wasn't over yet. He scanned the field for any sign of the opposing team, his eyes darting back and forth as he dodged and leaped to avoid any incoming tackles. Then, out of the corner of his eye, he noticed Aurora flying fast in his direction. He could feel his pulse quicken as he tried to come up with a plan to evade her.

But just when he thought all hope was lost, he noticed Jafari coming up behind him, his cheetah-like speed on full display. Ethan raised his hand with the flag to the side, and Jafari grabbed it without skipping a beat. Ethan could feel the weight of the flag lifting off of his hand as he watched Jafari race towards their team's field, a look of determination on his face. It was a thrilling moment, and Ethan couldn't feel prouder of his team and their incredible abilities.

As Jafari reached their team's field, the rest of the team cheered and clapped, their excitement palpable in the air. Emma and Alex ran over to Jafari, high-fiving him and congratulating him on a job well done. Willow was also there, a wide grin on her face. Isabella came short after, celebrating as well. Together, they stood there for a moment, catching their breath and reveling in the rush of the game. It had been a hard-fought battle, but in the end, they had emerged victorious.

The players from both teams gathered near the center of the field, breathing heavily but with huge grins on their faces. They were all congratulating each other on the game they had just played, and even the Stone brothers had a smile on their faces.

"Good game, guys," Finn said, extending his hand towards Ethan. "You really made us look like fools back there."

Ethan shook Finn's hand and smiled. "Thanks, man. You guys gave us a run for our money too."

The rest of the players echoed Finn's sentiment, and there was a general feeling of camaraderie and goodwill in the air.

Remy, who had taken some of the hardest tackles during the game, chuckled and said, "I never thought I'd get taken down by an ant. You surprised me, Alex."

Alex grinned, puffing his chest out proudly. "I may be small, but I'm strong!" he said, flexing his muscles for emphasis. Emma playfully tousled his hair. "Don't let it go to your head, little guy," she said with a smile.

"Hey, that was pretty fun," Aurora said, grinning. "Anyone want to go again?"

The others laughed, but then they all nodded in agreement. "Yeah, let's do it," Jake said, grinning at his brothers. "We're not gonna let you guys win two in a row though."

The players split up into their respective teams, and Isabella took a moment to approach Ethan. "Nice moves out there," she said, giving him a smile. "I have to admit, I was a little nervous when you took the flag from me."

Ethan felt a rush of pride and excitement at her words. "Thanks, Isabella," he said. "But I couldn't have done it without you guys. Everyone played so well."

As they all got into position for the next round, Ethan felt excitement and anticipation for the next round. The last game had been amazing, he never felt so alive and he couldn't wait to see what the next one would bring.

CHAPTER 20

TRAGEDY STRIKES AGAIN

The last weeks of fall at the Sanctuary were crisp and clear, the air filled with the scent of woodsmoke and the sound of crunching leaves underfoot. The sun shone down on the colorful landscape, casting a golden glow over the rolling hills and forests. The students spent their days exploring the lush wilderness, taking in the beauty of the changing leaves and snapping photos of the wildlife that surrounded them.

In the evenings, they would gather around the campfire, roasting marshmallows and sharing stories. Mr. Black, and sometimes George, regaled them with tales of his adventures in the Animalian world, and the students listened with wide-eyed wonder. The nights were cool, but the warmth of the fire and the laughter of their friends kept them cozy and content.

As the days passed, the leaves continued to fall, painting the ground in shades of orange, red, and gold. The students knew that winter was coming, but they didn't mind. They were in no rush to leave the Sanctuary.

On the next day, a Sunday, Ethan, Marcus, and Emma decided to spend the day outside, enjoying the last few weeks of fall playing frisbee in the fields. After having breakfast, they left the cafeteria and were on their way to the fields when they saw Michael walking past them. Michael, who was usually a reserved and studious young boy, had tears streaming down his face.

Ethan, Marcus, and Emma were taken aback by the sight of Michael crying and immediately went to him to see what was wrong. Michael, who was short and chubby, with short, dark hair that was always unkempt and a somewhat big nose, tried to wipe away his tears and compose himself. He was not outgoing, but was always willing to talk if someone approached him.

"Michael, what's wrong?" Ethan asked, concerned.

Michael explained that he had received some bad news that morning. "It's Elmer," he replied, his voice breaking. "He's gone."

A brief silence filled the air. "What do you mean?" Emma asked, her own eyes filling with tears.

"He died," Michael explained, his voice trembling. "After weeks of being unconscious because of the poisoning, he passed away."

The trio were devastated. They knew how much Michael loved Elmer, the baby elephant who had been his dear friend.

They could see the pain in Michael's eyes, and their hearts ached for him.

"I'm so sorry, Michael," Marcus said, placing a comforting hand on Michael's shoulder.

"Is there anything we can do to help?" Emma asked, wiping away her own tears.

"We're going to have a funeral for Elmer. Just be there for me and Elmer," Michael replied, sniffing. "That's all I need."

"Of course, we'll be there," Emma said, giving Michael a comforting hug.

The group stood there for a moment, in silence, as they mourned the loss of Elmer and offered their condolences to Michael. It was a somber reminder of the ongoing investigation and the cost it was taking on their loved ones.

The funeral was held in the animal sanctuary on the outskirts of the academy. The sun was shining down on the lush green fields, casting a warm and comforting glow on the solemn gathering. Ethan, Marcus, Emma, Michael, Sarah, Isabella, Aria, Alex and Ms. Rodriguez arrived early, along with a few other students from the academy. Some were able to dress in somber black and stood together in a small group, paying their respects to the late Elmer.

As they waited for the ceremony to begin, Ethan noticed that the animals of the Sanctuary were also in attendance. Birds perched on branches, watching the proceedings with curious eyes. Deers, rabbits and squirrels gathered at the edge of the field, their heads bowed in mourning. Even Talon came and landed on Ethan's shoulder.

When the time came for the ceremony to begin, Michael stepped forward to speak. His voice was filled with emotion as he spoke of Elmer, his dear friend and companion. "Elmer was more than just an elephant, he was a true friend. He had a kind and gentle spirit, and he will be deeply missed by all of us."

As Michael spoke, Ethan couldn't help but notice Braveheart standing in the distance, watching the ceremony with a somber expression. He wondered if Braveheart was truly mourning the loss of Elmer or if there was something more to his presence.

Ms. Rodriguez also gave a speech, her parrot perched on her shoulder. "Dear friends and family of the Sanctuary, we gather here today to say goodbye to a beloved member of our community. Elmer was a symbol of hope, joy, and love. He brought a smile to everyone who met him, and his gentle spirit will be missed by all who knew him."

The students, staff, and animals of the Sanctuary stood silent, tears streaming down their faces as they listened to Ms. Rodriguez's eulogy. She went on to describe Elmer's birth, his journey to the Sanctuary, and the special bond he had formed with the people and animals around him.

"Elmer was a reminder of the beauty and goodness that can be found in this world, even in the darkest of times. He was a shining light in a world that often seems so dark, and he will continue to live on in our hearts and memories. May we all strive to live our lives with the same kindness and love that Elmer brought into our world."

The group stood in silence for a few moments, letting the weight of Ms. Rodriguez's words sink in. Then, one by one, they each approached the pit to say their final goodbye to

Elmer, laying flowers and leaving small trinkets in his memory.

After the ceremony was over, the group dispersed, each lost in their own thoughts and memories of Elmer. As they walked away, Ethan had a feeling of sadness and a sense of loss. He knew that Elmer would always hold a special place in their hearts and that they would never forget the love and friendship the little animal brought to his friends.

As Emma, Marcus and Ethan walked back from Elmer's funeral, a heavy sadness hung in the air. The bright sunshine and chirping birds felt out of place in the wake of the young elephant's tragic death. The three friends walked in silence, each lost in their own thoughts and grief.

Finally, Marcus broke the silence. "If Elmer died from the poisoning, the coyotes and eventually Ms. Park will also die if nothing is done," he said, his voice heavy with emotion.

"But what else could we do?" Emma asked, her voice barely above a whisper.

Ethan noticed that Mr. Black wasn't present in the funeral, which was strange. He remembered overhearing Mr. Black and Braveheart's conversation and wondered if there was a connection.

"Maybe we should talk to Mr. Black," Ethan suggested. "He might have more information now or a plan."

"Yeah, that's a good idea," Marcus agreed. "We should go check on him."

The three friends quickened their pace. As they walked, Emma turned to Ethan and asked, "Do you think Mr. Black is allying with Braveheart?"

Ethan shook his head. "I don't know, I still trust him, but I hope we find out soon."

As they approached Mr. Black's office, they could see that the door was closed. They knocked softly and called out his name, but there was no response. Cautiously, they pushed open the door and stepped inside.

Ethan's heart felt heavy as he saw the signs of a struggle in the room. Papers were strewn about, as if someone had been frantically searching for something. The desk drawers were left open, revealing their contents scattered across the floor.

"Something's not right," Marcus said in a hushed tone, his eyes darting around the room.

Ethan nodded, his own fears confirmed by his friend's words. Ethan's heart skipped a beat. Lying on the ground near the corner was a large figure, motionless. He took a deep breath and approached the figure lying on the ground. As he got closer, he could see that it was indeed Mr. Black, their favorite teacher and mentor. Emma let out a shocked gasp and Marcus immediately called for help.

Ethan knelt down beside Mr. Black and felt for a pulse. It was weak, but it was there. He let out a sigh of relief and turned to Emma. "We need to get him to the infirmary. He's been poisoned, just like the others."

Marcus exclaimed in distress and Emma nodded, grabbing Mr. Black's arms and helping Ethan lift him up. As they carried him out of the room, Ethan felt a sense of dread in the pit of his stomach. This was not a good sign, and he feared that the worst was yet to come.

CHAPTER 21

THE ROAD TO REVELATION

On Monday morning, the headmaster, Braveheart, called for an assembly in the school auditorium, summoning all students and faculty to attend. As the students filed into the auditorium, a heavy tone of dread hung in the air. The news of Elmer's death and Mr. Black's poisoning had spread like wildfire, and many students were calling their parents to arrange for an earlier return home. Emma, Marcus, and Ethan sat together, discussing the events of the previous day.

"Maybe this proves Braveheart isn't guilty," Emma said. "I don't think he would hurt Mr. Black."

Marcus shook his head. "Or, Mr. Black finally found the truth of his crimes and confronted him, causing Braveheart to poison him too."

Ethan nodded, a solemn look on his face. "Yeah, it doesn't look good for Braveheart... but now that the piece of paper is gone we have even less evidence against him."

As Braveheart stepped onto the stage, the room fell into a hushed silence. The headmaster looked tired and worn, but his usual confidence and bravado still there. He cleared his throat and began to speak.

"I know that many of you have heard about the recent tragic events that have occurred at our school," he began. "I want to assure you all that we are doing everything in our power to investigate and get to the bottom of what has happened. I understand that many of you are worried and scared, and some of you may even want to return home."

A murmur of agreement rippled through the crowd. Braveheart paused, taking a deep breath before continuing. "In light of these recent events, I have made the difficult decision to close the school early before the holidays break. We will be transporting students outside of the Sanctuary today and tomorrow. I understand that this is not the ideal situation, but the safety and well-being of our students, staff and animals is of the utmost importance."

As murmurs of concern and surprise rippled through the crowd, Braveheart held up a hand to silence them. "I understand that this is not the news you wanted to hear, but I assure you that we are doing everything in our power to resolve these issues. We will be conducting a thorough investigation into the poisoning, and I have full faith that we will find the person responsible. We will work hard to get the

Sanctuary back to normal and hopefully, we'll be able to reopen on the beginning of the new year. The school will keep communicating with the families either way. I want to thank you all for your patience and understanding."

Finally, Braveheart gave a hopeful closing remarks "I know that we will come out of this stronger and more united than ever before. Together, we can overcome any obstacle. Let's take care of each other and support one another as we navigate this difficult time. Thank you."

As Braveheart finished his speech, the students began to file out of the auditorium, their minds buzzing with questions and concerns. Emma, Marcus and Ethan looked at each other, unsure of what to say.

They sat in silence, each lost in their own thoughts. The weight of the recent events, the death of Elmer and the poisoning of Mr. Black, hung heavily over them. Finally, Marcus spoke up, his voice heavy with defeat. "I guess that's it then," he said.

Ethan, determined to not give up, spoke up. "We can't just give up," he said.

But Emma interjected, "What else can we do? At least now people are going home and will be safe."

Ethan's determination didn't falter. "But what about Ms. Park and Mr. Black? And the Sanctuary, will it be closed down forever? We can't allow that!"

Marcus, understanding the gravity of the situation, replied, "We're with you buddy, but we're just teenagers. We can't take on Braveheart without proof."

Ethan sat there, feeling defeated and overwhelmed. Marcus stood up, a determined look on his face. "I'm going to find Sarah and get her phone number before she leaves," he said, turning and walking away. Emma looked at Ethan with a compassionate gaze. "I'm sorry, Ethan," she said softly. "I have to pack up stuff from my dorm. I'll see you later, okay?" She stood up and walked away, leaving Ethan alone with his thoughts. He sat there in silence, feeling hopeless. He didn't know what the future held for the Sanctuary, for Ms. Park and Mr. Black, or for himself. He had finally found a place where he felt like he fit in, and now it was slipping away.

As Ethan walked down the hall, he passed by George, who was moving at his usual slow pace. "Hi Ethan," George said, "excuse my fast pace." Ethan chuckled at the old man's dry sense of humor.

"How are you today?" Ethan asked, slowing down to walk beside him.

"I'm well, my boy," George replied. "And yourself?"

"I've been better," Ethan said, sighing. "It's been a tough couple of days, with Elmer and Mr. Black."

George nodded sympathetically. "Indeed, it has. But we must remember that the past shapes us, and it's important to learn from it."

"I know that," Ethan said. "But it's hard when the past is so closely tied to the present, and the future is so uncertain."

"I understand, Ethan," George said, patting him on the back. "But we must keep moving forward, and always look to the past to guide us. It's the only way we can make sense of the present and shape a better future."

Ethan nodded, taking in George's words. "Thanks. I'll try to remember that."

"Of course, my boy," George said, smiling. "And if you ever need anything, don't hesitate to come find me. I'm always here to help."

Ethan thanked George and continued on his way, feeling a little bit better with the old man's wise words in his head.

Ethan had a sudden realization, and quickly made his way to the library. As Ethan walked through the library, he noticed that it was almost empty. Only a few staff members were present, busily organizing books and shelves. He made his way to one of the computers, where he knew he could access a vast amount of information about Animalian history and events.

He began searching for "Braveheart" and to his surprise, he couldn't find anything particularly negative about the headmaster. Instead, he found articles and reports praising Braveheart for his leadership and dedication to the Sanctuary and its inhabitants. He read about the many improvements and renovations that Braveheart had implemented during his tenure, and how he had always put the welfare of the animals and staff first. Ethan couldn't believe what he was reading and wondered how he missed all these good things before.

Ethan found several articles and records detailing Braveheart's past accomplishments. One of his biggest challenges had been leading a defense against a group of rogue elephants Animalians who were terrorizing nearby villages. Braveheart had assembled a team of skilled animal warriors, including a pack of wolves with enhanced speed and agility, and a group of bears with immense strength and endurance. Together, they were able to defeat the rogue elephants Animalians and restore peace to the region.

Another victory for Braveheart was his successful negotiation with a group of bird-like Animalians who had taken control of a major air transport hub. Braveheart had used his own powers of persuasion and his extensive knowledge of Animalian culture to convince the leaders of the bird tribe to relinquish control of the hub and work towards a more peaceful resolution.

Suddenly, he noticed something that made him pause. He picked up an article and started reading, feeling a rush of excitement as the pieces of the puzzle started to fall into place. The words on the page made everything crystal clear, and Ethan's mind raced with the realization of what he had discovered. He read on, jumping from article to article, making connections and piecing together the information he had learned so far. The more he read, the more he understood why the school was in danger and why the poisoned beings were suffering. He was horrified by the truth, but he also felt a sense of determination. He knew what he had to do.

Ethan's heart raced as he quickly gathered his things and left the library. He had to tell Marcus and Emma what he had learned. They had to act fast if they were going to save the school and the lives of the poisoned beings. He ran through the hallways, his mind racing as he tried to organize his thoughts. He needed to be clear and concise when he spoke to his friends, so they could understand the gravity of the situation. He couldn't let the Sanctuary and the lives of his friends be destroyed. He needed to make them understand that they had to act now.

Ethan burst through the door of his dorm room, ready to share the information he had just uncovered in the library. "Marcus! You won't believe what I..." he started, but his words were cut off as he saw his friend sitting in a chair, bound and gagged. Panic set in as he realized that something was very wrong. As he took a step further into the room, the door slammed shut behind him with a loud bang, making him jump in shock. He quickly turned to see Braveheart standing behind him, a sinister grin on his face.

CHAPTER 22

BATTLE FOR SURVIVAL

Ethan's heart was pounding in his chest as Braveheart stood before him, a towering figure of power and authority. The leader of the Sanctuary, the man who had always been a source of guidance and protection, now stood before him as a ruthless killer.

"It was about time you arrived, Ethan," Braveheart said, a cold smile on his face. "I was just chatting here with our friend Marcus about how close you got to catching me. I can't allow that to happen."

Ethan took small steps back, his mind racing as he tried to process what was happening. "Why are you doing this?" he asked, his voice trembling.

Braveheart's expression turned cold, and he looked at Ethan with a hint of confusion. "Why am I doing this? I need to kill you so you don't spill my secret," he said, his voice low and menacing.

Ethan's courage grew as he realized that Braveheart was not the all-knowing, all-powerful leader he had thought. "No, I'm asking why did you poison the animals, and then Ms. Park and Mr. Black?" he asked bravely.

Braveheart looked confused for a moment, as if he was trying to remember why he had done what he had done. "Is that the part where I'm supposed to explain my evil plan?" he laughed, a hint of madness in his eyes. "Hm... I don't know, maybe I got mad. Who cares! Now, I brought a little present for you boys," Braveheart said, holding up a small bottle filled with a green liquid. "Don't worry, it will be painless and quick, unless you prefer the painful way," he said, cracking his knuckles. He took a step forward, and Ethan noticed that he was limping.

Ethan knew that he had to act fast if he and Marcus were going to survive. He stood tall and confident, a smirk playing on his lips as he looked at Marcus. "Don't worry, Marcus," he said. "Braveheart is on his way to save us," Ethan bluffed.

Marcus's eyes widened in disbelief. He had never seen Ethan like this before, and he wondered if his friend had lost his mind. Braveheart, meanwhile, stood frozen, as if shaken by Ethan's words. He tried to regain his composure and keep his voice commanding and threatening. "What are you talking about?" he growled. "I am Braveheart!"

But Ethan was undeterred. He stood bravely, his eyes shining with determination. "No, you're not," he said. "I've been reading about how the real Braveheart chased a criminal to a crocodile den, and the only thing that was found of the criminal was his leg. It turns out the criminal was a chameleon Animalian who could shape-shift and regrow limbs. His name was Leon. You're Leon. You didn't die that day, you let the crocodiles take your leg to mislead everyone."

As Ethan spoke, he noticed someone outside the dorm, peering through the keyhole. With his falcon eye he realized it was Emma, she must have come to help them pack and leave the school. But as she listened to everything she was waiting for the right moment to help.

Ethan continued, his voice gaining momentum. "You disguised yourself as Jack and poisoned Elmer, probably to test the venom on a powerful animal like an elephant. Then you poisoned the coyotes to see if either the animals or Doug could detect the venom with their keen sense of smell, but they didn't, so you continued with your plan."

"I remember Mr. Black telling us how he had wronged you," Ethan continued. "But his relationship with Ms. Park, whom you had feelings for, only made your thirst for vengeance even stronger. You poisoned her, probably to savor your revenge, and she tried to leave a note with your name on it, but she couldn't finish writing it."

Braveheart stood there for a moment, a sinister smirk spreading across his face. He threw his head back and let out a maniacal laugh, the sound echoing through the room. Ethan watched in horror as Braveheart's body began to morph, the transformation taking place in a matter of seconds. When the transformation was complete, Ethan was staring at a man he had never seen before.

Leon was tall, with a lean and athletic build. His dark hair was styled in a messy, yet sophisticated manner, giving him a menacing appearance. He had piercing green eyes that seemed to bore into Ethan's soul, making him feel as if he was being dissected by a machine. Leon's cold and calculating demeanor was a stark contrast to Braveheart's warm and confident presence.

"Looks like I underestimated you, Ethan," Leon said, his voice dripping with disdain. "Park's note was actually a blessing in disguise. I was planning to poison Braveheart too, but when I found out you were strongly suspecting him, I figured I would help with this narrative. After all, having him locked up for life would be much more satisfying than just killing him."

Marcus's muffled moans filled the room as Leon stood before him, a twisted smirk on his face. "I thought I had everything figured out," Leon said, his voice cold and menacing. "I gave Braveheart a powerful sedative toxin, so I could come here as him and kill one of you. The lucky one to stay alive would be the witness against Braveheart, but you had to go and be clever, didn't you, Ethan?"

Marcus struggled against his restraints, trying to speak through the gag in his mouth. But Leon simply laughed, a cruel and joyless sound. "Now, both of you will die," he declared, his green eyes gleaming with a sinister light. "You'll be nothing more than a footnote in my grand plan."

As Leon advanced towards Ethan, the young falcon Animalian called out, "Emma, now!" In an instant, the bear girl jumped out from behind the door and tackled Leon from behind, attempting to immobilize him.

Ethan was right behind Emma, jumping in to help with a swift sweep kick. The kick caught Leon off guard, sending him crashing to the ground. But the battle was far from over. Ethan and Emma struggled to hold onto the slippery Leon, their hands slipping from his thrashing body as he released a potent toxin into the air.

The two friends immediately felt the effects of the toxin, coughing and feeling lightheaded. Despite their valiant efforts, the toxic fumes weakened their grip, allowing Leon to slip away and regain his footing.

With a smirk on his face, Leon taunted them, "You two are much stronger than I expected, but still no match for me." Ethan and Emma stood side by side, ready to face Leon once again. They both knew that this was a fight to the finish, and they were not going to give up until they had taken down this dangerous foe.

As the three of them clashed in battle, Ethan and Emma valiantly charged forward, their fists flying and legs kicking as they aimed to take down the dangerous Leon. The former student of the Sanctuary was a formidable opponent, dodging and weaving with lightning speed as they threw punches and kicks in his direction. He knew that he needed to stay out of Emma's reach, for her brute force strength would be too much for him to handle. On the other hand, Ethan was nimble and fast, making it difficult for Leon to land a hit.

Despite their best efforts, Leon was eventually able to catch Ethan, wrapping his arm around the boy's neck in a tight rear naked choke. He looked at Emma triumphantly, and declared, "It's over!" with a cruel smirk spreading across his face. Emma's heart raced as she realized the dire situation that her friend was in.

Suddenly, Talon flew through the slightly open window, he swooped down with ferocity, striking Leon in the face with his sharp claws. The attack caught Leon off guard and he stumbled back, clutching his eye as he groaned in pain. The distraction was enough for Ethan to slip away and regroup with Emma.

With Leon momentarily disorientated, Emma seized the opportunity to strike. She pulled back her fist and with a fierce roar, she launched it forward with all her might. The punch connected with Leon's chin, sending him crashing to the ground, unconscious.

Ethan quickly moved to untie Marcus, who had been gagged and bound throughout the entire altercation. As Marcus was finally freed, he rubbed his sore wrists and looked around, taking in the chaos that had just occurred.

"Well," he quipped, "I guess I won't be getting my nap in today." The others chuckled at Marcus' quick wit, grateful for a moment of levity amidst the tension.

They tied Leon up and made their way towards the headmaster's office. Marcus felt compelled to express his admiration for Ethan's detective work. "Good job putting all these pieces together Ethan," he said. "I bet even Sarah would be impressed by that."

Ethan replied with a chuckle, "Thanks, but it would be for nothing if Emma wasn't there to kick this guy's butt!"

Emma, who was carrying the unconscious Leon over her shoulder, blushed slightly at the compliment. "You were not bad either Ethan, but you should really thank Talon," she said, glancing at the falcon resting on Ethan's shoulder. "He is the one who saved your life."

Talon made a series of chirps and screeches that sounded like a joyful reply. They were all proud of their work, having put an end to the chaos and bringing the culprit to justice.

As the trio arrived at Braveheart's office, they found him just coming out of the haze of the sedative toxin that had put him to sleep. He gazed at the young Animalians, looking completely bewildered. Emma placed Leon on the ground, and Braveheart's expression changed as he saw who was tied up in front of him. "Leon! I thought he was dead! Black tried to warn me, but I couldn't believe it," Braveheart exclaimed.

Ethan took a step forward, eager to explain what they had uncovered. "Turns out he's been infiltrated in the school for a while. His plan was to kill one of us while disguised, to place the blame on you," he said. Marcus handed Braveheart the bottle with the green liquid that Leon planned to use.

Braveheart held the bottle up, examining it carefully. "This is amazing work, you three. We're going to lock him up for his crimes, and now that we know what we're dealing with," he said, holding the bottle aloft, "we'll be able to develop an antidote in no time."

Ethan's face lit up with hope. "Does that mean we don't need to close the school?" he asked. Braveheart smiled at him kindly. "We're still going to close early for the holidays, just to sort all this out, but if everything goes according to plan, we'll be back in the new year like nothing ever happened," he replied. This was a great comfort to the students.

Braveheart turned to the trio and thanked them for their help. "In the name of the Sanctuary, I want to thank you. Your help will never be forgotten," he said. And with that, Braveheart took charge of Leon, leaving Ethan, Emma, and Marcus to enjoy the holidays and the knowledge that they had saved their school and solved a mystery.

CHAPTER 23

FAREWELL

As Ethan, Emma, and Marcus sat in the infirmary of the Sanctuary, watching over their friends who had fallen ill from the poison, they decided to make the most of their extra time at the school. They chose to stay at the Sanctuary for a couple more days. With only a handful of students left, they had the opportunity to enjoy each other's company and have some fun.

"So, what do you guys want to do today?" Ethan asked, eager to make the most of their time together.

"I've always wanted to try archery," Emma replied, a glint of excitement in her eyes. "Maybe we could go to the shooting range?"

Marcus nodded in agreement. "That sounds like a great idea. I'm in too."

The trio made their way to the shooting range, where they spent the morning practicing their aim and challenging each other to friendly competitions. They laughed and cheered, completely absorbed in the moment. Obviously, Ethan with his falcon sight was unbeatable.

As they made their way back, they discussed the events of the past few days. "Can you believe how far we've come?" Marcus said, a note of wonder in his voice. "I never would have thought that we'd be saving the school and the people in it."

Emma smiled. "It's been a wild ride, but I wouldn't have wanted to do it with anyone else."

Ethan nodded in agreement. "Me neither. We make a pretty good team."

The trio saw Sarah coming out of the library. As she approached them, Marcus' heart raced. He quickly greeted her, "Hey Sarah! What are you still doing in here?" Sarah replied, "Hey guys! I was about to board the bus when I heard the news about Leon being captured. So I decided to stay a few more days to use the library and get ahead on my assignments. By the way, good job cracking the case and catching Leon. That was very courageous of you three."

Ethan jumped in, "Yeah, and we couldn't have beaten Leon without Marcus here. He was really, uh, bound to help in the fight," he said with a smile. Emma held back a giggle as she watched the interaction between Marcus and Sarah.

Feeling a mix of embarrassment and excitement, Marcus replied, "Oh, it doesn't matter. I mean, we all did our part." Trying to steer the conversation away from himself, Marcus then said, "So, uh, Sarah. Would you like to join us for dinner? I mean, if you're not busy or anything."

Emma and Ethan suppressed their laughter as they noticed the redness creeping up Marcus's neck. Sarah smiled warmly. "I'd love to, thank you for the invitation."

As soon as Ethan entered the cafeteria, he noticed Jack sitting in a corner, all by himself. Jack had a brooding look on his face, with his arms crossed in front of his chest. His green eyes seemed to be staring into the distance, deep in thought.

Ethan quickly excused himself from his friends and made his way over to Jack. "Hey, Jack," he said as he approached the table.

Jack looked up at Ethan, his expression guarded. "What do you want?" he said, with a hint of superiority in his voice.

Ethan took a deep breath and looked Jack in the eye. "I came to apologize," he said, trying to sound friendly. "What we did, accusing you like that, was wrong. I just want to say I'm sorry."

Jack's expression changed from one of suspicion to surprise. "Oh, well, it's no big deal," he said, trying to sound casual. "Forget about it."

Ethan smiled warmly. "Do you want to join us for dinner?" he asked.

Jack hesitated for a moment, then nodded. "Sure, why not?"

So, the five teenagers sat down at a large table in the cafeteria and enjoyed a meal together. Despite the awkward start to their conversation, they all ended up having a good time, laughing and chatting about the events of the day. It was a reminder that, no matter what their differences may be, they could all come together and be friends.

As the bus pulled up to the school, Emma, Ethan, and Marcus gathered their things and made their way outside. The air was crisp and the sky was a beautiful shade of blue. They looked at each other, feeling a mix of sadness and excitement. They had spent the past few months together, delving into the mysteries of the Animalian world, studying its creatures, cultures and history, and working hard to solve the mystery of the poisonings and now, it was time for them to take a break of all that.

"Well, this is it," said Emma, looking at her friends. "I can't believe our semester is already over."

"Yeah, it went by so fast," replied Marcus, who was also feeling emotional.

Ethan was about to reply when they heard someone running towards them. It was Mr. Black, the teacher who had also been affected by the poison.

"Wait! Wait for me!" he called out, appearing as strong and lively as ever.

"Mr. Black! You're okay!" exclaimed Emma, clearly surprised to see him.

"Yes, I'm fine now. And Ms. Park and the coyotes are also recovered," he said, beaming with happiness. "I just wanted to say goodbye and thank you all for what you did. You three were incredible, figuring out that it was Leon who was behind everything, even though I never shared my suspicion."

The three friends were stunned. Mr. Black had been so close-lipped about his suspicions, they had no idea that he suspected Leon too.

"Wow, thank you Mr. Black," said Ethan, still processing the information.

"Yeah, it was a team effort," added Marcus, modestly.

As the bus pulled up, Mr. Black gave them one final goodbye and wished them a safe journey home. They hugged him, grateful for his words, and boarded the bus.

The trip home was filled with reminiscing about their time at the Sanctuary and the events that had transpired. They talked about the lessons they had learned and the bonds they had formed. They knew that their time at the Sanctuary would always be a special memory, one that would stay with them forever. And they couldn't wait to go back.

EPILOGUE

The jail cell where Leon was being held was made of strong iron bars, with a small opening in the front for food to be passed through. Leon sat on the small bed in the corner of the cell, his eyes fixed on the door as Mr. Black approached.

"Leon," Mr. Black said, his voice deep and steady.

Leon looked up, his green eyes filled with anger and hatred. A big fresh scar located near his left eye. "What do you want?" he spat.

"I came to apologize," Mr. Black said, holding up his hands in a peaceful gesture. "I know I made mistakes in the past, and I am sorry for the pain I caused you. I shouldn't have done a lot of those things to you and I deeply regret it."

"Apologize? Sorry?" Leon sneered. "You think apologies can make up for what you did to me? You think sorry can make up for all the years I spent feeling alone and ostracized?"

"I understand that," Mr. Black said, his voice calm and patient. "But we can work to make things right. We can work to heal the wounds of the past."

"No," Leon said, shaking his head. "I will never forgive you. I will never forgive any of you. You took everything from me, and now I will take everything from you."

"Leon, please," Mr. Black said, his voice growing more urgent. "You have to let go of this anger and hatred. It will only lead to more pain and suffering."

"I will never let go," Leon said, his voice filled with venom. "I will never forgive you. I will never forget. I will make you all pay for what you've done to me."

Mr. Black sighed, looking at Leon with a mixture of sadness and regret. He had tried to reach out, to make amends for the past, but it was clear that the wounds were too deep to be healed.

"I'm sorry, Leon," Mr. Black said, turning to leave. "I hope someday you can find peace and forgive us for our mistakes."

And with that, Mr. Black left the jail cell, leaving Leon alone with his thoughts of anger and revenge. Leon yelled from his cell, "This isn't the end, Bob! It won't be over until every last one of you is gone! Every, last, one!"

ABOUT THE AUTHOR

Gustavo Carvalho was born and raised in Salvador, Brazil, where he grew up surrounded by a passion for video games and fantasy books. Although he never quite realized his dream of becoming a video game developer, he has never lost his love for the imaginative worlds that he grew up with.

From an early age, Gustavo found himself drawn to movement and physical expression. When he turned 16, he fell in love with parkour, a passion that has stayed with him throughout his life. Soon after, Gustavo made the decision to become a vegetarian, driven by his compassion for animals, a choice that he has maintained for over 15 years.

After finishing college, Gustavo moved to California in 2015 with his wife and son, where he worked as a programmer. Following years writing for computers, he decided to write for humans.

Now a father of two young sons, Gustavo has written his first book, The Sanctuary's Revenge. He wrote this book with the hope of creating something that his children would love, and that would inspire their imaginations and encourage them to see the world as a place filled with wonder and adventure.